Dear Reader,

I'm a bad person. No, really. You see, I'm a card-carrying buttinski. That means I pretty much like managing things. And people. Although I swore up and down I was *not* the "managing" grandmother character in *To Marry at Christmas* (Silhouette Romance), written to commemorate my older daughter's courtship and wedding, everybody who knew me just sort of snickered and said, "Yeah, sure."

These same people will know that, in *A Bride After All,* Marylou Smith-Bitters might just bear a teeny-tiny resemblance to yours truly yet again.

I can't help it. I like to see everyone happy. And if any two people ever deserved a little nudge (and *needed* a little nudge!) toward their Happily Ever After, it's Claire Ayers and Nick Bennington.

Please come on along and meet Claire and Nick, and the adorable Sean, and if you've any romance in your soul (and I know it's there or you wouldn't have picked up this book in the first place, right?), root along with me, er, Marylou, as they discover that love is a leap of faith worth taking.

All the best to you!

*Kasey Michaels*

# A BRIDE AFTER ALL

## KASEY MICHAELS

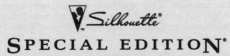

**SPECIAL EDITION**

Published by Silhouette Books

America's Publisher of Contemporary Romance

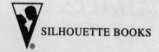

**SILHOUETTE BOOKS**

Recycling programs
for this product may
not exist in your area.

ISBN-13: 978-0-373-65529-8

A BRIDE AFTER ALL

To Buttinskis everywhere—and you know who you are!

## *Prologue*

Nick Barrington shifted uncomfortably on the nicely upholstered chair built for a woman, not a man who easily topped six feet, and believed he could now empathize with an elephant stuck in a Waterford's Crystal showroom.

If he moved wrong, breathed wrong, he believed he might set off some sort of chain reaction that would end with this pretty room turned upside-down.

To his left was a glass-topped case loaded inside and out with doodads and thingamajigs and lacy garters and rhinestone tiaras and—why did that book have lace on the cover?

The bow window behind him was decked out in lace curtains that had—what were they called? Oh yeah—swags on them, their hems dragging on the floor. The rugs were flowered, the tables all had spindly, curvy legs. And if he looked to his right (which he kept trying not to do), someone had fitted out a mannequin with some sort of corset and tiny panties that made the damn thing look like some guy in town for a business convention should be buying it a cocktail.

Now where had that come from? It was a curse, being a writer, even if his work was confined to straight news at the *Morning Chronicle*. Maybe he had a second career in lurid fiction just waiting out there somewhere for him?

Just as he took another sneak peak at the mannequin, Chessie Burton, who had introduced herself as the owner of Second Chance Bridal, popped into the room via a door painted ivory, its architectural detail picked out in gold gilt.

"Still hanging in, I see. I should have stickers here for men who venture in. You know, like they give kids after the doctor gives them a shot? They could say *I survived a visit to Second Chance Bridal*," she said, opening the door of a large credenza and then pulling a can of soda from the small refrigerator hidden behind the doors. She tossed it to him. "There you go. Drink it, press the cold can to your aching forehead. Whatever works best for you. She won't be too much longer. I think she's found her dress. We just need the perfect headpiece. And here it is."

Nick smiled weakly as Chessie opened the glass

case and took out a mini-wreath of pink rosebuds and ribbons and returned to the dressing room.

He popped the top of the can, hurried to drink the fizzy soda that immediately began bubbling out the opening thanks to Chessie having thrown the can at him, managing to only spill some of the liquid on his shirt, and not anything perishable.

Still, for all his discomfort, Nick wouldn't be anywhere else right now. Not when Barb had specifically asked him to be here.

His cousin had been through hell for the past six years, ever since Drew had become a casualty of the war. She'd crawled so far inside her grief she'd nearly disappeared. But now there was Skip, and God bless the man, because he loved Barb with all of his huge heart.

Nick hadn't realized how badly he'd missed Barb's smile until Skip had come into her solitary life and dared her to live again.

If his cousin wanted Nick to not only escort her down the aisle, but to do it wearing that dumb wreath on his head, he was her man.

He looked up as he heard Barb call his name, to see her walking toward him, and immediately got to his feet, first carefully putting the soda can on a crystal coaster on the table beside him.

He'd called her Tinker-Barb when they were kids because she'd been so tiny, her masses of blond ringlets seeming almost too heavy to be supported by her slim, fragile neck. She was all grown-up now, tall and willowy, but still fragile in appearance, with a heartbreaking, ethereal beauty usually reserved for fairies and wood sprites.

Somehow, the gown she was wearing captured the essence of her, the gentleness of spirit that had drawn the big guy to her. Skip was Barb's protector, and she was his cherished queen. Nick believed he had never seen such a soft, perfect love.

"Somebody's going to have to scoop Skip up with a spoon when he sees you," Nick teased her as Chessie helped Barb manage the too-long skirt of the gown as she stepped onto a low platform in front of the three-way mirror.

Nick knew nothing about gowns. He couldn't have described this one in print if given a year and a stack of fashion magazines to help him. All he knew was that the material was...filmy. Slightly pink. It had some narrow, trailing ribbons on it, and some of those small pink rosebuds stuck to some of the ribbons. The wreath thing was on her head, and her blond curls hung in ringlets and small, sort of fuzzy curls that softened her pixie face.

He wouldn't have been surprised if Barb turned around and there were gossamer wings stuck to her back.

"What do you think, Nicky? I...I think I like it. No, I think I love it. Chessie says it will be perfect for an outside wedding at the Rose Gardens, like we've planned. You know, with the gazebo and everything? Nicky? Say something."

Nick was at an unaccustomed loss for words. His eyes stung with unfamiliar tears. He raised his hands, gestured helplessly, said "Ah, jeez, Barbie," and wrapped his arms around her.

"I think he approves," Chessie said, laughing as she pulled a tissue from somewhere and began dabbing at her own eyes. "You guys are fun. Oh— hi, Marylou, you showed up at just the right time. Come see our latest bride."

Nick disengaged himself from his cousin's embrace, kissed her on the cheek, and then stood back to allow the new arrival to see Barb in her gown. He wanted to refuse the tissue Chessie surreptitiously handed him, but then took it, grinning at her and feeling foolish, yet extremely happy.

"You picked the perfect name for your business, Chessie. My cousin has *second chance* written all over her face. And she deserves one. Thank you for putting what I guess is the crowning touch on her happiness."

"Well, isn't that just the nicest thing to say," the newcomer said before extending her hand to him. "Hi, Marylou Smith-Bitters, two-time patron of Second Chance Bridal, and frequent visitor because Chessie doesn't throw me out. Do I know you? I think I know you. No, wait, don't answer. I'll figure it out. Besides, I want to meet this gorgeous creature. She looks like something out of a Renaissance painting, doesn't she?" Marylou walked completely around Barb, who couldn't seem to stop smiling. "I wouldn't be shocked to hear a knock on the door and open it to see a unicorn eager to lay down at your feet, sweetie. You're pretty as a picture."

"Thank you, Ms. Smith-Bitters," Barb said, turning to admire herself in the mirror.

"No, thank *you*. I never come in here that my faith in humanity isn't revived. Chessie's a genius, not that she didn't have a lot to work with. Why I—" Marylou swung around, eyes narrowed, pointing a finger at Nick. "I remember now. You teach at the community center every Tuesday and Thursday evening, right? Oh, of course that's right. I'm always right."

Nick switched from elephant-in-a-crystal shop to butterfly-pinned-to-a-board. Or maybe deer-caught-in-the-headlights. Marylou Smith-Bitters was well and truly in the category of *one of a kind*. Fortyish, or at least she looked fortyish, she was tall, slim, had a mop of perfectly arranged light brown hair that would probably not move in a hurricane, and sharp green eyes that obviously never missed a trick. She had that put-together air that comes with amazing self-confidence, and if she broke into a song and dance she'd probably be great at both, as there was something vaguely theatrical about her.

"Guilty as charged, Mrs. Smith-Bitters. I teach English as a second language to new immigrants."

"That's very nice of you," Chessie said, motioning for Barb to bend her knees so that she could remove the wreath from her head.

"Keeps me off the streets," Nick said, faintly embarrassed. He turned to Marylou. "I'm sorry I don't recognize you, Ms.—"

"Marylou," she interrupted him. "I thought Smith-Bitters had all sorts of cache, you understand, and the towels are all embroidered, but I wish I'd thought about it a while longer before I did it. Smith-Bitters, Smith-Bitters. Sounds like a cough drop, doesn't it? Or perhaps a new cocktail? I'll have a Smith-Bitters on the rocks, please, with a twist of lime. And you probably didn't recognize me because I only took over the registration desk last week when the girl I replaced went on maternity leave. Seven-pound, six-ounce boy. She named him Rodrico Estaban Beinvenido. The Third. Isn't that a lovely name? You have a son, don't you? Is he taking a class as well, or does your wife work nights and you just bring him along?"

It was all very neat, and extremely friendly and disarming, but Nick still got the feeling that Marylou Smith-Bitters would have made a hell of an investigative reporter. To reward her, he gave her what she wanted to know.

"Sean is taking karate, yes. He loves it, which is good because I'm divorced, his mother is totally out of the picture, and, at nine, he hates babysitters but is too young to stay home alone."

Marylou's laugh tinkled like little bells stirred by a gentle breeze. "Handsome, eligible *and* smart. You left out your age and occupation, but I can look those up, I'll bet. Very good, Nick."

"There she goes again—the matchmaker." Chessie had turned Barb over to a teenage assistant who escorted her back to the dressing room, and was now frowning at Marylou. "You'll excuse her, Nick. I think it's time for her medication."

"That's okay," he said. "I'm used to it. My sister, who thankfully lives in Cleveland now, keeps signing me up for those online dating services. But just for the record, I'm not interested, thank you. Sean and I are doing pretty well on our own. Oops, there goes my cell," he said as the phone in his pocket began playing the Philadelphia Eagles fight song. "Please excuse me, and if you'd tell Barb I'll be waiting outside for her? Nice to meet you both. And Chessie—thanks."

The door had barely closed behind Nick Barrington when Chessie turned on Marylou. "No. Don't."

"I don't have the faintest idea what you're talking about." Marylou went to the cabinet and pulled out a bottle of low-calorie water. "Ever wonder why we drink this, when water has no calories at all? Americans, the ultimate consumers." She twisted open the top and took a long drink. "But it is good, I'll give them that. I wonder what it would do, mixed with Scotch. I really can't acquire a taste for Scotch, and it's Ted's favorite."

"Forget the water, forget the Scotch. Don't forget Ted because he's a doll and you don't deserve such a great husband. Mostly, forget Nick Barrington."

"I've got it. He's a reporter for the *Morning Chronicle*. When you said his full name like that, I remembered seeing his byline. He did a great four-part series on domestic violence a few months ago, remember? He writes like he really cares. Yes, he's perfect."

"No man is perfect," Chessie protested, collapsing into the chair lately vacated by Nick. "Ask me, I'm the expert, and have the scars to prove it."

Marylou waved away Chessie's words with a graceful shooing motion, the three-carat ring on her third finger left hand catching the sun and shooting off mini-rainbows in the air. "As if Rick Peters is any example of mankind. The guy is pond scum, so he doesn't count. And if you'd let me—"

"Not even if you had George Clooney's private phone number," Chessie said, grinning. "Okay, so I might make an exception for George. But seriously, Marylou. You don't really mean you're going to try to find Nick Barrington a wife. He clearly doesn't want one."

"That's because he doesn't know any better."

"Proving my point—there is no perfect man."

"Don't confuse me with logic," Marylou said, trying to frown. She didn't quite get there, which was what happened when she got her regular botox injections in her forehead. "Did you see him, Chessie? He was *crying*. Not all sloppy, like those wimpy touchy-feely sorts, but the way a really caring man cries. It was just so honest—so *real*. Not a question in my mind—he's a keeper. Some lucky woman is soon going to be very grateful I don't listen to you."

Chessie leaned forward and rubbed at her frown-crinkled, botox-free brow. "Here we go again. People are soon going to think I send you out to bring in customers. Not that we deal with second-chance grooms."

Marylou laughed, and then clapped her hands. "Yes, that's it. Second chance for Nick, second chance for her."

"Her who? And why am I asking? Because I don't want to know. I'm sure I don't."

Rolling her eyes, Marylou said, "Oh, stop, you know you're dying to hear. I was bored last week at the registration desk. I mean, I love volunteering, you know it's my thing…"

"And you've got nothing else needing nipping or tucking and you already own more clothes and jewelry than Macy's or Lord and Taylor, so you have the free time…"

"Okay, I'll give you that one. Although I am considering a butt lift." She turned her back, presenting her posterior to Chessie while looking over her own shoulder to peer at her reflection in the three-way mirror. "At fifty, gravity starts to win, you know. Not that I look anything close to fifty."

"Fifty-six. Remember those three kamakazies you had at Elizabeth's wedding reception? You confided in me then."

"That was a great wedding, wasn't it? But onward and upward. *Upward*—get it? Do you think I need a butt lift?"

"I refuse to answer on the grounds that I'd probably completely lose it if you walked in here one day carrying one of those blow-up rubber doughnuts to sit on. Now, please, let's change the subject. And not back to Nick Barrington, either. Eve will be finished measuring Barb for a hem, which is really all that gown needs, and my bride could come walking out here at any time to overhear you cackling and see you stirring your cauldron while you make plans for her cousin."

Marylou shrugged. "All right. I was just saying that there was nothing much to do at the registration desk last week, so I started a conversation with this other volunteer who I think would be perfect for—"

"Stifle yourself. Here she comes. Let me write up the sale, and then we'll go get some lunch."

"And I can tell you all about Claire Ayers. Just the sweetest girl. Divorced, although I don't know any of the details."

Chessie got to her feet just as Barb walked into the room. "And I'll listen, God help me, because I'm as sick and twisted you are."

"Yes, I know. It's why I love you." Marylou obediently sat back in her chair, took another drink from her bottle, and began planning her opening move for Tuesday evening. Nick Barrington would never even know what hit him…

## Chapter One

Claire Ayers pulled into the parking lot of the community center with ten minutes to spare before facing a classroom filled with parents eager to learn how to best care for their children. As the physician assistant in her brother Derek's pediatric practice, Claire spent a lot of her time dealing with concerned parents, but with her class it was a little different.

Many of them barely spoke English. Many had come to America never having seen the inside of a doctor's office. They provided her with a challenge she didn't face in her brother's practice.

But all of the parents she saw had one thing in common. They all loved their children and wanted what was best for them. She admired them all, so much.

Not that she saw children anywhere on her own personal horizon. She had, once, when she and Steven were first married, but that dream had disappeared along with the marriage. Then again, Steven had been enough of a child himself to not want competition from some sweet-smelling adorable infant.

Claire hadn't thought about Steven in months, or their home in Chicago, or the life she'd had there. But he'd phoned her today, to tell her he was getting married again. Had he thought he'd needed her permission? Or maybe he'd just wanted to rub it in. *See? Other women find me lovable. I told you it was you, not me. You're the one with the problem, babe.*

Maybe this time Steven had found the right woman for him. One who was content to be Steven's wife, and nothing else, no one else. He was very, very possessive. Claire hadn't seen that side of Steven when they were dating, but once they were married, everything had changed. When she'd been late to dinner because of an emergency at the pediatric office she worked in, or tried to share a story about something that had happened during her day, or sought his comfort when parents had been forced to hear frightening news about their child, Steven's only answer had been, "Quit. I need you more than they do. I don't see marriage as a part-time job, damn it."

Not for her, anyway. He'd never think that *he* should quit his job and stay home so that he'd be there when she got home. But Steven was a real "I'll get the meat, you keep the cave warm" kind of throw-back, with an increasingly frightening penchant for jealousy that had her rushing home from work, mentally preparing her apologies.

She'd stuck it out for six months, even if the marriage had been over only a few weeks into it.

It had been difficult, admitting that kind of defeat, and especially so early in the marriage. But the day she'd spotted his car behind her, following her from the office to the supermarket, had put the topper on it for her. She'd moved out the next day while he was at work, leaving behind everything except her clothes and most personal possessions. He could have the house, the furniture, all the wedding presents. She just wanted out, needed to be out, before Steven took the next step in what was clearly a poisonous situa-tion—physical violence.

She'd called her brother, flown to Allentown on the first flight out, and begun working in his office the following Monday after finding a furnished apartment in nearby Bethlehem. She'd given Steven everything in the divorce, and then taken back her maiden name.

Life went on, or so they said, and she was deter-mined to get on with hers.

Except she probably hadn't. Gotten on with her life, that was.

So now, three years later, while Claire was pretty much still treading water, Steven was getting married again. Well, good for him. Maybe he'd changed, wised up. Or maybe this marriage would be strike two. Steven and his bride-to-be were not her concern.

Which didn't mean Claire hadn't considered calling the girl and giving her a friendly heads-up, except for the fact that women in love rarely listened to soured ex-wives.

Claire flinched as someone knocked on the side window of her car. She'd been sitting there, her hand on the key that was still in the ignition, wasting time she didn't have to spare.

She turned and smiled at Marylou Smith-Bitters, who had now stood back to give her room to open the car door. Claire had first met Marylou last Tuesday, when she'd helped translate for a new member of her parenting class who still needed to formally register. Not that Claire's Spanish was very good, but it was infinitely better than Marylou's, which was pretty much limited to ordering sangria and paella.

"Hi, Marylou. Hang on a sec," she said as she exited the car, and then opened the back door to extract her purse and briefcase. She reached back to grab Susie, the infant CPR mannequin she'd borrowed from her brother's office.

Marylou looked at the mannequin, a smile curving around her collagen-enhanced lips (not that Claire could tell—but Marylou had confided in her when they'd gone for coffee after class was dismissed). "Is that the new way to carry infants? By the ankle?"

"Susie doesn't mind," Claire told her as they fell into step and headed for the front door. "She doesn't even mind when students smash all her ribs trying to resuscitate her. You will hear the alarm go off if you're passing by the classroom, though, so don't let it throw you."

"Very little throws me, Claire. Running out of my favorite lipliner. Popping an acrylic nail ten minutes before leaving for some evening event Ted insists we attend. The mere thought of my cosmetic surgeon retiring to Boca. Alarms don't faze me."

Claire laughed, as she knew she was supposed to do. Really, though, she couldn't help liking Marylou. The woman was rich, pampered and totally upfront about all of it, even poking fun at herself. And she was very sincere about giving of her time and money because she had both, plus a genuine interest in the people around her. What was not to like? Even if she had found herself telling Marylou things—like about her divorce from Steven—when she had always made it a point to keep her private life private.

Some people just had that knack for getting others to talk about themselves. Marylou Smith-Bitters had it in spades.

They entered the building together and walked down a hallway crowded with students heading for classrooms.

"Uh-oh, I seem to have a line at my desk," Marylou said, sighing. "How about this—Ted is in Palm Springs for some golf outing and I'm alone, with no reason to go home. Are you free to meet me in the cafeteria after class for some caffeine and deadly white sugar?"

Claire gave a moment's thought to her small condo and the empty refrigerator in the galley kitchen. "Sure, although I think I'll stick to my usual caffeine-free soda and a couple slices of pizza. Thanks for asking. See you later."

Marylou was looking past her. Busy-busy, that was Marylou. "Good. Great, it's a date." She put her hand on Claire's upper arm and almost pushed her aside. "Excuse me, there's somebody I want to corral before classes start. See you in the cafeteria."

Claire turned around to see Marylou approaching a man she'd seen last week. And last month. And during the spring session. He was the kind of man you didn't miss, even if you weren't looking.

Tall, sandy-haired in that casually mussed style she had always found intriguing—making her palms itch to run her hands through the hair falling onto his forehead and push it back into place while hoping it would fall forward once more so she could do it again.

He dressed casually, but casual looked good on him. As did his smile, currently aimed at Marylou.

What didn't look good on him was the eight- or nine-year-old boy he brought with him every Tuesday and Thursday. She hadn't seen a wedding ring (because she'd looked), but that didn't mean anything. Idle curiosity had made her check, nothing more.

One, she didn't date. Two, he might be married.

Three, men with kids were often looking for a mother for those kids, and she wasn't interested in being dated for her mommy potential.

Claire turned and walked toward her classroom, stopping only twice to look back at Marylou and Mr. Casual.

Not that she was interested.

The food court in the community center was well stocked, but the aroma of pizza was always what got to Claire, so much so that she didn't even have to place her order anymore. Ruth, the woman who manned the counter, automatically served her two plain slices and fished a bottle of caffeine-free diet soda for her from the cooler.

Was that good or bad, being so predictable?

Her purse and briefcase hanging from her shoulder and Susie clasped by the left foot and dangling upside-down, Claire hung onto her tray and stood in the middle of the crowded tables and chairs, looking for Marylou.

"Claire! Over here!"

Claire turned toward the sound of Marylou's voice. Her smile froze on her face, because Marylou wasn't alone at the table in the corner. Mr. Casual was sitting there, too.

"Oh, Marylou, what are you doing?" she grumbled under her breath, and then squared her shoulders and headed for the table. "Hi, I guess I'm late," she said as she slid her tray onto the tabletop and then divested herself of her belongings. Susie was cute, and helpful, but she was also heavy. "Hello," she said to the man across the table as she sat down.

Then, to keep her hands busy, she opened her bottle of soda and took a drink from it. Her mouth had gone rather dry.

"What? You two don't know each other?" Marylou asked as if shocked. "I would have thought—haven't you both been teaching classes here forever?"

"Third semester."

"This is my second year."

The first answer was from Mr. Casual, the second Claire's own, delivered at the same time. "Sorry," Claire added, trying to ignore Marylou's soft kick under the table.

"Oh, no, no, don't apologize," Marylou said, beaming. "Because now you're going to know each other, aren't you? Claire Ayers, please allow me to introduce Nick Barrington. Nick, my friend Claire, who teaches a parenting class here. Nick teaches English as a second language." She picked up her coffee cup and smiled at them both from above the rim. "There, that was easy. All done."

"Hello, Nick," Claire said, extending her hand halfway across the table. "It's nice meeting you."

"Back at you," he said, taking her hand. His eyes were green, now that she could see him up close. And they were laughing. Like he knew what was going on and found it all extremely amusing.

Claire clenched her teeth even as she continued to smile. That way maybe nobody would know that the touch of his hand had done something strange to the region of her stomach, but she probably would be able to keep from throwing up her first sip of soda.

Marylou put down her cup and actually rubbed her hands together. "Nick has a son, you know. Sean. He's over there, at that big round table with all the other kids from his karate class. Aren't they all just so cute in their white pajamas?"

"The uniform is called a *karategi*, Marylou," Nick said, clearly suppressing another smile. "If Sean heard you calling his uniform pajamas he'd be highly insulted. He's up to his red belt now, with the brown one coming next, if he qualifies." He looked at Claire. "Karate is supposed to foster the spirit to overcome life's obstacles, along with instilling courage, respect, self-confidence, self-control, and self-discipline. I'm still waiting for those last two to kick in, but he's getting there."

"How old is Sean?"

"Nine, going on thirty-five, which makes him older than me and means sometimes he thinks he's the parent and I'm the child."

"I think I remember reading somewhere that the children of single parents often mature quickly," Marylou slipped in neatly as Claire felt another soft kick on her ankle. "But you'd know that, wouldn't you, dear, working with children all day. Claire's a physican assistant for her brother, who's a pediatrician," she told Nick, turning to look at him, her eyes wide and innocent. "It's all very...very medical," she ended rather weakly, then flashed another smile.

The woman's cell phone, which was on the table next to her, rang, and Marylou snatched it up like a drowning man grabs a life ring thrown from a friendly passing ship.

Claire kept her eyes on her plate as Marylou spoke rather breathlessly into the phone. "Yes? Yes? Oh, no! Well, of course, Chessie, I'll be right there. No, no, no problem at all. It's not like you wanted your battery to go dead, now did you?"

The cell phone snapped shut and at last Claire looked up again, to see Nick Barrington sitting with his chin in his hand, his eyebrows cocked in a way that made her want to laugh as he listened to Marylou explain how she had to leave, she really did, but please just stay and talk to each other while Claire finished her pizza.

Which could take a while, as Claire's appetite had disappeared about three minutes earlier.

Marylou gathered up her sweater and purse and blew kisses to both of them before hurrying out of the food court in her three-inch heels.

"Well, that was subtle," Claire managed when she could find her tongue.

"You noticed? But I think her intentions are good. At least I hope so. You aren't a secret ax murderer, are you?"

"Not so much so that I list it on my resume, no," Claire said, beginning to relax. Nick's smile had that sort of effect on her, as did his voice, which wasn't too deep, wasn't too personal or flippant, but just right. If he were one of the Three Bears, he'd be the one whose voice was *just right*. And why was she thinking about fairy tales?

"Fair enough. How's your ankle?"

"My—it's fine."

"Good. Mine is all right, too, although it was pretty hard not to flinch when she gave me the last little nudge under the table before she took off. Those shoes of hers come to a pretty deadly point."

"Like I said—subtle. And then that convenient call from her friend, so that she had to leave us here alone. But I think you're right, and she meant well."

"I met Marylou last week when my cousin was looking for a wedding gown, but didn't realize she volunteered here. The woman who phoned her is Chessie Burton, the owner of Second Chance Bridal. Nice girl, but I have a feeling she's probably sitting at home with her feet propped up on the couch as she watches TV, and not stranded on the highway with a dead battery."

Claire picked up a slice of pizza, her appetite inexplicably back. "True. Unless this Chessie person is a method actor and is even now standing on the side of the thruway, feeling ridiculous. So, you teach English as a second language. How does that work? Do you speak several languages?"

"Two—three if you count my attempts at English. I learned Spanish in college, and picked up French at home as a kid. My mother's French. Other than that, we all just sort of muddle through the best we can. Tonight we worked our way through t-o, t-o-o, and t-w-o. At the end of the class, the consensus was that English has been made difficult on purpose and that as a nation, we should be ashamed of ourselves."

"Did you point out that English came to us from Great Britain?"

Nick spread his hands. "Immaterial. They're not in England, they're in America, land of the free and home of the dollar menu. Which was my first mistake."

"How so?" Claire noticed she'd somehow downed both slices of pizza, but she still had soda left, so she could be excused for lingering.

"Well, tonight we role-played going to a fast-food restaurant to order a meal."

"From the dollar menu."

"Exactly. My students need practical English. They're not going to be dining at top restaurants, not at first anyway, although I believe they all plan on that sort of success, and more power to them. Anyway, I had them role-play going *to* the restaurant and ordering *two* burgers, and then adding that they wanted a bag of fries, *too*."

Claire tried not to giggle. "Okay, I think I see the problem. They really wanted only one bag of fries, so why should they say they wanted two?"

Nick ran his fingers through his hair, and some

of it fell back down over his forehead. Claire stopped breathing.

"I finally changed the last one to *also,* when I realized the problem. But I think they thought I was cheating. Plus, it only got worse, thanks to the student playing the guy behind the counter."

Claire raised her hand, waving it like an eager student. "Wait, wait, let me figure out how it got worse. You be the student, and I'll be the bored teenage clerk behind the counter."

Nick scratched at his ear, as if considering her offer. "All right. Maybe then I can figure out how to do this without having my students tossed out of the restaurant. Which, as it stands now for a few of them, is a distinct possibility."

"Good," Claire said, sitting up straight and holding out a hand as if poised over a cash register. "Hello, and welcome to Claire's. May I take your order?"

"Yes, thank you. I would like two hamburgers. I want an order of fries, too."

Claire began punching imaginary buttons on her imaginary ordering machine. "Got it, that's two burgers, two fries. Would you like something to drink with that? Our milkshakes are on a two-for-one special today until two o'clock. Would you like to have two?"

"Yes, thank you. Two."

Claire kept punching imaginary buttons. "Okay. So that's two hamburgers, two fries, four milkshakes. That'll be seven dollars and twenty-two cents."

"You know, looking at you, with that pretty honey-colored hair and those big brown eyes, I never would have taken you for a sadist," Nick said, shaking his head. "The order is wrong, Miss. We need to fix it, please."

She bit her bottom lip for a moment, feeling silly and just a little bit delighted with herself. "Sir, I'm only recording what you're telling me. And there's a line forming behind you and I go on break soon. If I could have your final selections? Two hamburgers, two fries—"

"No, no! Two hamburgers, and one fries *also*. And I will be happy to have two milkshakes, too, for the cost of a single one, thank you."

"But you said you'd have two milkshakes too."

Nick half rose from his chair. "Never mind, I'm not hungry."

Claire gave up her pose and cupped her chin in her hands. "Your poor students. They're all going to starve to death."

"I wrote up notes for the students who were still having problems, to use until our next session, so they won't starve. Although they might get pretty sick of hamburgers and fries between now and then. And now, since I've been dying to ask—what's with the doll?"

Claire looked over at their table companion. "Bite your tongue. Susie is far from a doll. She's a complex and highly sensitive CPR mannequin I borrowed from my brother's office. And I think I did better than you did tonight. Only three people fractured her little infant ribs. Poor Ivan, he has hands like hams, and alarms went off on his first compression. He was devastated. Next session, we investigate the wonderful world of devices for taking a child's temperature."

Nick made a comical face. "I think I can still remember how my mother took mine."

Claire felt hot color run into her cheeks. "We have other ways."

"That's good to hear. With Sean, I mostly stick to the back of my hand pressed against his cheek while I'm touching my own at the same time. So far, I'd say the method has been at least ninety-five percent effective. He's hot, I call the doctor. He's coughing, I call the doctor. He throws up on my shoes, I call the doctor. All the gals at the desk know my voice. But, you know, being in charge of a kid, all by yourself, is a pretty heavy responsibility. I don't take any chances."

This was probably the perfect opportunity to ask Nick where his wife was, Claire knew, but she couldn't bring herself to do it.

Luckily, he seemed to sense her curiosity. Or was that unluckily? She didn't want to seem eager. She didn't want to be another Marylou. One Marylou was definitely enough.

"Sandy left us when Sean was three," he said quietly. "You're probably used to hearing this, but the marriage was a mistake. I loved her, she loved the idea of singing in a band, someday making it to the top. When Sean…happened, we married, thought we could make it work. But we never could master juggling, keeping all the different balls in the air. Sandy's totally out of Sean's life, which was her choice. To tell you the truth, I don't even know where she is, although I did get a postcard from Reno about six months ago with the photograph of a small night-club on the front and her note on the back. 'Here's our latest gig—great, isn't it?' That was it. She didn't even ask about Sean."

"I'm sorry," Claire said quietly. "It couldn't have been easy for you. For any of you."

"It was hell, for a long time," Nick said, and then shook his head. "I'm sorry, I don't know where that came from. On the lighter side, Mommy and Me days at nursery school were interesting. But good or bad, we manage in our own way. Sean's a good kid, very adaptable. And, speaking of Sean, I think it's time the two of us hit the road."

"Oh, yes, of course," Claire said, quickly piling napkin and soda bottle on her tray and standing up along with him. "It was very nice meeting you."

Nick laid his hand on her forearm. "That's not going to do it, you know."

She looked down at his hand, a sudden flash of her ex-husband's proprietary way of always keeping a hand on her making her uncomfortable, but the hand was already gone. "What…what's not going to do it?"

"You and me, sharing coffee and chat in the community center cafeteria. Marylou will consider her mission a failure."

"Her mission?"

"Oh, yeah. I have an aunt like Marylou. Aunt Beatrice. She won't be happy until she thinks she's set the table for a grand romance."

The color was back in Claire's cheeks. "I'm...I'm not interested in a grand romance. My career takes up a lot of my time."

"Well, good, because I'm not either. Interested in a grand romance, that is. I've got Sean, my job, these night classes. My own plate is pretty full, too. Or is that also? I never got that far into grammar with my classes; in the beginning, it's enough they learn what they need to know to get around town, use the phone, read street signs. Plus I'm lazy, which is why God created editors and proofreaders. I should brush up, huh?"

Claire smiled. "Now you have even more on your plate."

"I do. And one other thing. For instance, my cousin is getting married three weeks from Saturday. That's how I met Marylou, remember, at the bridal shop. Barb hadn't thought she should wear a gown for a second wedding, but Skip and I finally talked her into it. Skip's her fiancé. Last-minute decision— the gown, not the fiancé—but Chessie said she could help her and she really did. Would you...would you, um, consider being my date for the wedding? It would be a huge help."

"Is Aunt Beatrice going to be at the wedding?" Claire asked, tongue-in-cheek. He really was charming, and he wasn't even working at it.

"I'm that transparent? Yes, she is. But if you go with me, that will make Marylou happy, and when Aunt Beatrice sees us, it will make Aunt Beatrice happy. It's a win-win situation, really. Because if Aunt Beatrice can be used as an example, Marylou is going to keep pushing us together and then rushing off to help a sick friend or something, and it could get embarrassing after a while."

Claire closed her eyes, sighed, thinking it was already pretty embarrassing, and she wasn't looking forward to Marylou's Second Act. And then she nodded her head. "It makes sense. And I do like weddings. As long as they aren't mine," she added, smiling. "But now I have to go, really. I need to stop by the hospital and check on one of my brother's patients. We started a new antibiotic this afternoon, and I want to see if there's been any improvement."

Nick took her tray for her, making it easier for her to load up her purse and briefcase and Susie.

"See you Thursday," Nick said, and then he headed for the trash cans. She watched as he separated the paper and plastic. Conscientious. Law-abiding.

And such a wonderful smile.

## *Chapter Two*

Thursday, a few minutes before six o'clock, Nick delivered Sean to his karate class and then returned to the front doors of the community center, telling himself he was only being polite, watching for Claire to arrive so that he could say hello to her.

Which was a bunch of hooey.

She'd really made an impression on him on Tuesday night. Why? He didn't know. Maybe it was something about that hint of sadness in her eyes. Maybe it was the wistfulness in her smile. Like she was a woman who had lived, and not all of that life had been sunshine and roses.

Maybe it was the journalist in him, always looking for a story.

Nah. His attraction to her had nothing to do with anything even vaguely professional, or even altruistic.

She was a beautiful woman. She affected him on a gut level, pure and simple. She was the face you spotted across a crowded room and just had to figure out a way to meet. His response to her had been pretty much hormonal.

And what was the matter with that?

Nick began a mental list: You haven't had a gut-level hormonal response to a woman in a long time. You don't have time for a romance. You have a son to raise. You have an ex-wife who pretty much soured you on following through on gut-level hormonal responses.

"Hi, you're looking intense. Still trying to figure out to, too, two?"

Nick turned around at the sound of Claire's voice, to be immediately struck once more by her beauty, her cool, polished appearance, and those too-human eyes.

"Hi, yourself," he said, smiling at her. She was tall, not as tall as him, but just a perfect height so that they'd fit together well on the dance floor, walking together, lying beside each other…"Um, no Susie tonight?"

"Nope, I'm on my own tonight. Just me and my selection of thermometers. Have you seen Marylou?"

"No, I've been lucky so far," he said, falling into step with her as they turned to walk down the wide tiled corridor. "Look, maybe I was out of line the other night, asking you to come with me to my cousin's wedding. If you want to change your mind, I'd understand."

"Are you sure? What about Aunt Beatrice?"

"Aunt Beatrice and every unattached female between the age of consent and Medicare eligibility she'll be introducing me to, you mean? Never mind, I rescind my offer for you to change your mind. It's the coward in me."

"Well, good, because I already bought a dress." Claire stopped in front of her classroom door. "Oh, now you should see your face. It's priceless. No, I didn't buy a dress. Nor did I pick out china patterns. But I did run into Marylou on my way in earlier, and she was all set to toss me at your head again—some idea about joining our two classes together since we're both dealing with some language barriers—until I told her we were going to your cousin's wedding together. She's off somewhere now, probably purring as she licks cream from her whiskers. Not that Marylou has whiskers, but you know what I mean."

Nick scratched at a spot behind his ear. "So we're taking the easy way out? Joining up out of necessity, in order to protect ourselves?"

"Please, all this flattery will turn my head," Claire said as she stepped aside, allowing a young woman to enter the classroom, bringing her closer to him, close enough that he could smell the slightly flowery fragrance of her hair. He liked the way she wore it, all pulled back from her perfect oval face. What was the style called? Oh, right, a French twist. Yeah, he liked it. He'd like taking out the pins and seeing how long her hair was, too. That could be interesting.

Mind-wandering over, he shot back to attention. "Ouch, sorry. It's hard to believe I make my living with words, isn't it? Because that was really clumsy."

"Yes, Marylou told me you're a reporter for the *Morning Chronicle.* I was very impressed. I even looked up some of your articles on the Internet. You're very good."

"And now I'm totally at a loss for words," Nick told her. "Thank you."

"You're welcome," she said.

And then they just stood there.

Looking at each other.

Now what? Had he really been out of the game so long that he'd forgotten the rules?

"Would, uh, would you like to meet in the cafeteria after class?" he asked her at last. "Sean likes to sit with his friends and see who can dribble the most chocolate ice cream down the front of their white *karategis.*"

"Sure, that would be fine. Well, it's that time, I guess."

Nick lifted his hand to give a small wave to her departing back, and then manfully fought down the impulse to find a way to kick himself all the way down the corridor to his own classroom. She had to think he was an idiot. *He* thought he was an idiot. And about as smooth as a centipede on roller-skates.

"Pretty lady, Signore Barrington. *Occhi molli di un Madonna.* Soft eyes of a Madonna. You should, how you say, snatch her up?"

"Thanks, Salvatore, I'll think about it," Nick told the squat, cheerful man who had come up beside him, still dressed in a white baker's uniform, as if he'd come directly to class from his job. "Hey, I told you, no more cannoli. You don't have to bring me presents."

"But I want *to* bring it for you. *Two* of them. And some pignolata, *too.* Your boy, Sean, he likes? Yes?"

"Yes, he does," Nick said, accepting the string-tied box because it was easier. And, well, because he liked pignolata, *too.* "How are your wife and the new baby coming along?"

Salvatore's English suffered a bit as he enthusiastically described his happiness in both his wife and his wonderful son, clearly the most beautiful wife and the most handsome, perfect baby. "And he is all-American, my boy is, one hundred and fifty percent. Now my Evelina and me, we must be one hundred and fifty percent American, *too.* Like our boy. And you, Signore Barrington, you are helping us. You are a good man."

Salvatore's smile was so wide, his heart so large, his eagerness to make a better life for his small family so evident. And people wondered why he volunteered at the community center? Let them meet Salvatore and the others just like him, these wonderful people with their hopes and their dreams—then they'd understand.

"Thank you, Salvatore," Nick said, genuinely humbled. "I'm only glad I can help. And you know, Miss Ayers teaches a class in child care, if you think your wife would be interested?"

Salvatore nodded his head furiously. "Signora Smith-Bitters, she already tell me. My Evelina, she will start with the classes next week."

"And the baby? Where will he be, if you're both here?"

Salvatore's smile disappeared and he looked down at his flour-dusted work shoes. "She said not to say."

"Who said not to say? Not to say what? Salvatore?"

"Signora Smith-Bitters," the man said, sighing. "She say not to worry. She say to bring Stefano with us, and she will find a way." He looked up at Nick. "What is this, this find a way?"

Nick turned to look down the corridor, to where Marylou Smith-Bitters was standing next to the registration desk, talking furiously while artfully arranging a neck scarf around the shoulders of a beaming young woman who had probably never before thought of a scarf as anything more than protection from the wind and rain.

One by one, and whether the person wanted it or not, clearly Marylou Smith-Bitters was out to fix—and even *fix up*—the whole world.

"There's a saying here in America, Salvatore," Nick said, draping an arm over the man's shoulders as they walked into the classroom. "Never look a gift horse in the mouth."

* * *

Claire stood in front of the row of sinks in the women's lavatory and contemplated her reflection in the mirror.

A few wisps of hair had escaped her classic French twist style, but all in all, she thought she still looked pretty well put together, hair-wise. It was simply easier to wear her hair up when she spent her days dealing with infants and small children who invariably had fists of steel when it came to grabbing on to and holding on to her hair as she examined them.

Her lipstick could use a touch-up, though.

She rummaged through her bag, not noticing Marylou's approach until the woman was standing next to her, leaning forward to dab a tissue at the outside corner of one eye.

"There, that's better," Marylou said, blinking a few times and then smiling at her reflection. "Non-clumping mascara. What a huge fib. Oh, that's a pretty shade," she added, taking the open lipstick from Claire before she could apply it to her mouth. "But not the best with that blouse, I don't think."

Claire looked down at her mauve-pink blouse, and then at the lipstick rapidly disappearing back into its tube. "It's not?"

"No, not really. There's a touch of blue to that shade. Better to go with a touch of gold. First thing we need to do is get rid of what's left on your lips, and then we'll go from there. You really should wear eyeliner, Claire, you know. A deep burgundy and chocolate sort of shade maybe, to accentuate your lovely brown eyes—make them pop—and then other colors if you want to be more daring. Not a lot, just a smudge, sort of smoky. Oh I know, you're young, and you're busy, but there's no excuse to not take a few minutes each day to pamper yourself. We call it the five-minute face now, or at least that's what the beauty experts call it. A little sheer foundation, a little light powder, some eyeliner and shadow, a touch of mascara, some color to the cheeks and lips."

The entire time Marylou was talking she was also rummaging in a cosmetic bag she'd pulled from her designer purse, handing Claire a moist towelette of makeup remover, a small pack of cellophane-wrapped makeup applicators of different sizes and shapes, a tube of lipgloss, an entire mini-palette of powder eye shadows—even a tweezers, which she quickly took back.

"Would you mind?" she asked, clasping the tweezers to her chest with both hands. "Just a little thinning, that's all. It will only take a moment."

"I…um…do I really need…?"

"I couldn't exist without my tweezers," Marylou said with the seriousness of a person commenting on the necessity of air to breathe. "Here, put all of that down and just let me play for a few minutes, all right? Because I've been dying to. You'll still have plenty of time to meet Nick in the cafeteria. Salvatore has his marching orders, and knows to keep him busy for a while."

"I guess it's good that one of us knows what you're talking about," Claire said, and then just gave in and went along…which was probably what most everyone did when faced with the velvet steamroller that was Marylou Smith-Bitters.

"There," Marylou declared the promised five minutes later, "all done. See? I told you it wouldn't take long. And what a difference. Take a look."

Claire obediently turned back to the mirror, and couldn't believe what she saw. Not that she didn't used to look like this. But that was years ago. Before the divorce. Before she had buried herself in her work and hoped that nobody would notice her because she'd been noticed enough, thank you, and didn't plan to be anyone's possession again.

"Oh, this isn't good, Marylou," she said, even as she admired how her eyes seemed to have new life in them. "I didn't look like this the last time he saw me. He'll think I've been…that I'm…"

"A woman?" Marylou supplied evilly as she stuffed cosmetics back into their assigned pockets inside her sophisticated bag that was, when you got right down to it, a feat of brilliant engineering on someone's part. "Now tell me why this is a bad thing."

"You know, Marylou, in some other generation, you'd have been burned as a witch. But thank you."

Marylou laughed, appreciating the joke. "You just go have fun, all right? Make Mama proud."

Claire lingered in the bathroom another few

moments after Marylou left, considering wiping off the makeup, but then decided against it. Because she did look good. She looked almost like her old self. Her younger self.

And it wasn't as if she hadn't thought of Nick Barrington at least a dozen times between Tuesday night and tonight. It was strange, thinking about a man. Thinking about him *that way*, at least.

"And what way is that?" she asked her reflection, and then quickly gathered her purse and briefcase and left the bathroom, because the only other occupant, who'd left the stalls to hear Claire talking to herself, was looking at her strangely.

She made her way to the cafeteria and got in line behind a group of women dressed in various styles of workout gear. Part of the exercise class held in the gym, no doubt. They all looked fit, toned, and happy to be filling their trays with fresh fruit and low-fat yogurt and sports drinks. Perfect tushes, perfect hips, perfect perky breasts.

"Here you go, Ms. Ayers, your usual," the server behind the counter said, producing an overloaded paper plate holding two slices of pizza.

"Thanks, Ruth," she said, feeling at least five pairs of feminine eyes on her, or on her pizza. Probably the pizza. "And my soda?"

"One caffeine-free diet cola, coming up."

The woman directly in front of Claire sniffed. "Whatever makes you feel better, I guess, huh? Five hundred calories a slice, but a no-cal soda. You're deluding yourself, you know. You're a heart attack waiting to happen."

"Is that so? My aunt weighs about what you do," Claire heard herself saying. "Eats well, exercises like a fanatic, and her last fasting bloodwork showed her total cholesterol coming in at over six hundred. Mine's one hundred and sixty-two. Do you know yours?"

The woman looked Claire up and down, sneered in her superiority, and turned back to her friends, leaving Claire feeling petty and ridiculous.

But really. Where was it written that everyone had the right to share their opinions with perfect strangers? What had happened to personal space, that invisible circle of privacy people were supposed to be allowed? When did everyone get so darned *interactive*?

She paid her bill, collected her change, and pretty much slammed her tray down on the table across from Nick before sliding into her chair.

"Damn, who stepped on your tail?" he asked her as she watched the women crowding around their round table, their mouths all moving at the same time, probably discussing the rude *fat* woman who didn't know any better. So they were probably all size two, or four, and she was a ten, sometimes a twelve. So what? And she hadn't had supper. This pizza was her supper. And they were small slices, nowhere near five hundred calories each.

Oh, God, she was losing it...

"I'm sorry, am I that obvious?" she asked him, dragging her gaze away from the table of women.

Nick looked to the same table, and then back at Claire. "Women like that scare me," he said, surprising her. "They always seem to travel in packs, and it's hard to tell one from the other. Like interchangeable dolls."

"Really," Claire said, her unreasonable anger disappearing as quickly as it had come. "What else scares you? Just in case I want to make a list."

He picked up his own slice of pizza. He hadn't had pizza on Tuesday. Maybe he hadn't been hungry on Tuesday. Maybe he'd ordered pizza because he thought she'd order pizza. Maybe she was thinking too much…

"What scares me? Let me think about that one. Okay, here's one—people who think they're always right."

Claire shot another quick look toward the interchangeable dolls. "Yes. You're right about that."

"Ah, but not about everything. I admit to my flaws. Just don't ask me to list them. My ego isn't that sturdy."

Claire smiled, now completely relaxed. He was so easy to talk to, to tease with. Almost as if they'd known each other for a long time. That was nice.

"All right. Mindful of your delicate ego, I'll give you one back, so we're even. Things that go bump in the night scare me."

Nick frowned. "You mean like ghosts? Goblins?"

She shook her head. "No, I don't believe in those. I mean sudden sounds I'm not expecting. Like the water heater having some sort of hiccup, or a branch scraping against the side of the condo, or a pot falling over in the dish drainer. Oh, and worst of all—an unexpected phone call after about eleven at night or before seven in the morning. Like that. I think I watched too many horror movies in my youth."

"Chainsaws and hockey masks," he agreed, nodding his head. "Sean stayed overnight at a friend's house last month and watched some damn DVD that gave him screaming nightmares for a couple of days. He won't be staying at that kid's house again for a while. So," he said, grinning at her, "you're a scaredy-cat."

She picked up her soda. "I prefer to think of it as having a vivid imagination. Still, I'm thinking about getting a dog. One that barks *really* loud at strange noises. The only problem is that I'm not home enough to care for a dog. It wouldn't be fair to the animal."

"We've got cats. Two of them, because I read somewhere that kids should have pets, someone else to be responsible for and confide in and all that good stuff. They sleep with Sean, but I somehow ended up with kitty litter and coughed-up hairball duty. The childcare books didn't cover that part well enough, I don't think. Do you want to go to dinner and a movie on Saturday night?"

It took Claire a few seconds to change gears from hairballs to movies. "Excuse me?"

He held up his hands in mock surrender. "Sorry. I sort of sprung that one on you, didn't I? But Sean's got a sleepover birthday party, and I thought well, I'll be at loose ends, and if maybe you'd be at loose ends, then we could—but you're probably busy."

"No," she said, shaking her head half in denial, half in amazement that she was saying what she was saying, "I'm not busy. I'll be on call for the hospital until four, but after that, I'm free. What…what kind of movie?"

Now his grin was downright evil. "I'm guessing horror movies are out?"

"I'm not going to live that one down in a hurry, am I? I think I need to know something else you're afraid of. Your first two were almost reasonable. Give me something irrational, so I can tease you, too."

He mumbled something she didn't hear because the exercise nuts two tables over had found something else to laugh too loud about.

"Excuse me? I missed that."

"The dentist, okay? I'm scared to death of going to the dentist. We're talking 'sedate the poor fool' kind of scared."

"Oh, my goodness. Really?"

"Really," Nick said, actually looking slightly pale. "You should have seen me the first day I took Sean to the dentist. The guy wanted me to sit in the chair and let him stick those damn probes in my mouth, to show Sean how simple it all was."

"Did you do it?"

"I did. Somewhere, there's an Oscar with my

name on it, because it was the acting job of the century. Now, are we even?"

Claire's curiosity was piqued. "Did you have an unfortunate episode at the dentist when you were a child? Because we see a lot of this in our practice. Some kids see a white coat and just freak out on general principle."

"Nope. Never had a bad experience. Never had a cavity, as a matter of fact. I just can't wrap my mind around voluntarily opening my mouth and letting some guy stick his fingers in it. It's unnatural."

"Oh, you poor thing," she commiserated, trying not to laugh. "If you think that's unnatural, wait until you hit your forties and your first prostate exam." And then, realizing she wasn't joking with her brother or any other medical professional used to speaking so plainly about the human body, she clapped her hands to her cheeks and exclaimed, "Oh, I'm *so* sorry. I shouldn't have said that."

But Nick didn't seem to mind. In fact, he was looking at her in real amusement. "You don't pull your punches, do you?" he asked her. "You know, that's nice. Much nicer than the usual getting-to-know-each-other-without-saying-anything-remotely-honest dance I'm used to on first dates."

"But this isn't a date. We're just having pizza in the cafeteria."

"Then maybe that's it. We're just two people, sharing a table and some conversation. Will going to the movies together screw it up, do you think?"

"I don't know. Do you think we should risk it?" Claire said as she noticed one of the pajama-clad students heading for the table. She recognized the boy, but saying so would only let Nick know she'd seen him enough, taken enough interest, to recognize his son. "I guessing that's Sean coming this way?"

Nick kept his gaze on her for a few moments longer, before turning to extend his arm, drawing his son against his side. "Hey, Slugger, are you ready to call it a night?" He pulled at the fabric of the *karategi* and gestured at the strawberry stains on the front of it. "What, they were out of chocolate?"

Nick's son was a miniature of himself. The same sandy hair, the same soft green eyes, the same wide smile, although Sean's teeth still seemed a bit too large for his mouth. He blushed at his father's teasing, dropping his chin a little, never taking his eyes off Claire.

Nick quickly made the introductions and Claire took the opportunity to stand up, gathering her belongings.

"I've got this," Nick told her, picking up her tray even as he grabbed his own and handed it to Sean. "Mind if we walk out with you?"

"That seems logical, since we're heading in the same direction," Claire told him, wondering if they were done discussing the matter of a movie on Saturday night. That might be good. It didn't *feel* good, but it was probably safer. Especially with Sean looking at her with such intensity.

They'd just stepped outside the building, dusk rapidly turning to darkness, when Nick's cell phone began playing, of all things, the Philadelphia Eagles fight song. "Excuse me," he said, flipping it open, frowning at the number, and then turning away as he put it to his ear.

Which left Claire and Sean to stare at each other.

"So," she said lamely (could she have been any more lame?), "you're taking karate lessons."

"Duh," he said, just like any smart aleck kid in a sitcom.

"I was trying to make polite conversation," she told him, not backing off. The kid was what, nine? She wasn't backing off from a nine-year-old. If she did that, she might as well quit her job and go work at a geriatric clinic, or something. "But we can just stand here and stare at each other, if that's what you want."

Sean looked at her a few moments longer, and then shrugged. "I can break boards with my bare hands."

"Okay, now that's impressive. And I imagine it takes a lot of concentration to do that?"

"Uh-huh, yeah," he said, turning his head when Nick said something into the phone, the tone of his voice clearly drawing his son's attention. "Dad?"

Nick raised a hand to him and continued talking.

"He sounds upset, doesn't he?" Sean asked Claire.

Now both Sean and Claire were listening, neither of them being very secretive about it, either. It was, if she chose to be an optimist about the thing, a sort of bonding moment for them.

"All right, yes, I understand. Fred, I said I understand how important this is. No, I know it can't wait for tomorrow, I know how these things are. I wrote the story, remember? Just let me think for a minute, okay? I've got Sean here and—let me call you right back. Just keep her on the other line. Do with her? I don't know—sing her a song, tell her about your trip to the Grand Canyon last month with Martha and the grandkids. Just don't let her hang up."

He closed the phone and walked back over to Claire and Sean.

"What did Mr. Abernathy want, Dad? Does he want you to go somewhere? I told you, I can stay by myself. Jimmy Peterson stays by himself all the time."

"Jimmy Peterson's parents are a sorry excuse for—never mind. You're not staying by yourself."

"Is there a problem, Nick?" Claire asked, once again stating the obvious. But at least he didn't say *duh* back at her.

"Just because Jimmy's mom let us watch that stupid movie—"

"Sean, quiet. Now, please," Nick said, running his hand through his hair as if the action might dislodge an idea he was searching for.

"Is Fred Abernathy your boss?"

"Managing Editor of the *Chronicle*. Damn. How do I say this? Claire—would you consider watching Sean for about an hour or so?"

Claire was rather proud of the way she managed

to not allow her eyes to pop straight out of her head as she answered, "Watch...watching him?"

"I know. I shouldn't ask. And I wouldn't, if this wasn't important. You see, I wrote this four-part series of articles a while ago—"

"On domestic violence and abuse," she interrupted. "Yes, I know. Remember I told you I looked you up on the Internet? It was, um, quite good."

"Thanks. The thing is, I got to know several of the women I wrote about. I mean, you try to keep your perspective, keep your eye on the story, but sometimes that isn't as easy as it sounds. Anyway, this one woman I profiled? God, why she stayed with the guy—I kept telling her she needed to leave."

Claire thought back over the articles she'd read, wondering if the woman was Maria, the mother of three who had, at last count, a total of sixteen broken bones over the past decade, all courtesy of her husband. Or maybe it was Lydia, the woman who wouldn't leave her abusive boyfriend because she felt she "deserved" his punishment when he was in one of his drunken rages. Or, worst of all for Claire, the unnamed wife who had to account for every moment of her every day or risk her husband's jealous wrath.

That one had hit too close to home, like a "this could have been you, if you hadn't had the family support to get out in time."

"Is...is she all right?"

"She is right now. The ER released her, but she's still there. Just a few bruises and a couple of cracked ribs, according to Fred, as if that isn't enough. I don't know about tomorrow, because her abuser will get out of lockup by then. She called the paper looking for me. She wants to go to a shelter."

"But that's wonderful. Why did she call you?"

He looked rather sheepish. "Because I gave her my number at the newspaper? I told her, any time, day or night, whenever, if she decided it was time to get out, I'd help her gather her kids and their belongings, personally get them settled into a shelter. Tonight seems to be her time."

"Then you have to do it," Claire said emphatically. "Now, while she's feeling strong enough, or frightened enough, to take that first step for herself and her children. But you have no one to keep Sean, do you? That's the problem."

"In a nutshell. Our usual sitter is on vacation this week. It could take an hour, a couple of hours, and I really don't want him to…you know. *See.*"

"No, of course not. I can take him for you, Nick. Get him home, get him to bed, wait for you." She managed a smile. "Remember, I deal with kids all day long, so I don't scare easily. I think we'll be fine."

"Dad? Can't I just go with you?"

Nick looked at Claire, his eyes searching her face. "Are you sure? I wouldn't ask, except that—"

"Just give me your address and a few directions," Claire told him. "Does he still need a booster car seat?"

"As if," Sean snorted, rolling his eyes.

Five minutes later, with Sean buckled up in the back seat—against his protests that he was tall enough to sit up front—Claire was driving through the darkening streets, wondering if her brother could recommend a good psychiatrist for her, because she had to be out of her ever-loving mind!

## Chapter Three

It was past midnight when Nick turned into the driveway leading up to the sprawling, white-painted red-brick ranch house on an outcropping of land overlooking the Rose Gardens in what was still known by the locals as the West End of Allentown. The white paint was old and worn, which was a look that had cost somebody a bunch of money, but went well with the trailing ivy and the slate-blue shutters and doors.

The house was built along a curve in the road, and the house curved along with it, with a fully excavated lower level that led out onto a series of flagstone terraces and steps down to a koi pond, a gazebo and yet another flagstone terrace. And trees. There were trees everywhere, planted to look natural, but not to block the view.

A kid in this house wanted to toss a ball around, he had to find a friend with a real backyard. But it was a beautiful yard, and anyone driving along the twisting macadam road that bordered the Rose Gardens could look up and be damn impressed, and probably think: wow, now there's a house!

The house and furnishings had been in the Barrington family for four generations. He'd bought the place, fully furnished, from his parents when they'd moved to Florida. Total cost: one dollar.

Repairs and maintenance on the house were separate, and pretty much non-stop.

What he'd always liked best about the house was his childhood bedroom, the one over the attached three-car garage, the one with the steeply pitched slate roof and vaulted ceiling, and the separate outside wooden staircase he'd used to his advantage enough times over the years that it would be a long time before he'd allow Sean to move into that room, if ever.

Nick cut the engine and remained behind the wheel, looking at the house, well-lit with ground lights and wrought-iron wall sconces, and wondered what Claire Ayers thought of his family homestead.

He hoped she wouldn't think he'd picked the décor. It suited him, maybe because it was home, had always been home; comfortable and faintly shabby, but in an old money sort of way; the furniture pretty ancient, but all of the best quality.

Sandy had hated the furnishings, had made fun of the flowered, overstuffed couches, the old-fashioned kitchen, but she'd also had no interest in redecorating, making the place her own. They'd spent the last two years of their married life in the house, yet there was nothing of her in it, nor had there ever been— something he'd realized shortly after she left for a weeklong tour with her new band, and never came back.

Because of Sean, because of Sandy, he'd never had another woman in the house. Not for six long years. Not until tonight.

"And she's probably wondering when the hell you're going to get out of the car and come inside, so she can go home," he told himself as he unhooked his seatbelt and opened the door.

The heady scents of bougainvillea and jasmine greeted him as he walked the curved slate path to the front door, passing beneath a squared-off wrought-iron trellis heavy with blooms. His grandmother had had a thing for bougainvillea. She'd left her mark, and the memory was a good one. It was a far different "welcome, come on in" than that of the women's shelter, which had smelled of pine oil and the large pot of chicken and noodle soup he knew from past visits was always simmering on the stove, "just in case."

He slid his key into the lock and stepped into the foyer. And stopped in his tracks. The place smelled like chicken and noodle soup. What the—?

"Hi," Claire said, stepping into the foyer. "This is the loveliest home you've got, Nick. I made some soup for Sean because he was hungry, and then joined him. It's just canned, well, two cans, so there's plenty left simmering on the stove. Do you want some?"

"Um…sure. Yeah, that would be nice."

"Good." She smiled at him, and he noticed she was wearing one of his mother's aprons. The one with the tiny pink rosebuds on it. She seemed to notice him looking at it, and quickly untied it, pulled it off.

"I'm sorry. I really look like I've made myself at home, don't I? But Sean has been in bed for hours, and I didn't want to wake him to ask him to explain the television remote to me, so I've been…well, I've got a thing for kitchens. Mine is this cramped little galley deal, so when I saw yours, it was like I'd stepped into heaven. I hope you don't mind that I…cleaned it up a bit."

Nick got a quick mental picture of how he'd left the kitchen as he and Sean raced off to the community center, piling the dinner dishes on top of the breakfast dishes that were still in the old-fashioned farm sink. "You didn't have to do that," he said, following her down the hall and into the kitchen. "Wow," he said once they were there and he was looking at the clean sink and uncluttered counters.

No stack of newspapers on the bar. No bags of corn chips or boxes of cereal out in the open because it was easier than putting them away. No small army of assorted superhero action figures or their vehicles and equipment littering the kitchen table. No dry cat food scattered on the floor around the cat dishes because Sean never seemed able to hit the dish and not the floor when he poured from the bag.

The entire kitchen seemed to…sparkle.

"It gave me something to do. I'm not good at having nothing to do, never quite mastered the art of sitting still and doing nothing. Derek calls it a failing, but since he's been able to have more weekends off since I joined his practice, he stopped complaining. Let me get you some soup, and then I'll get out of your way."

"Only if you have a cup of coffee with me before you go," Nick told her, pulling out a chair at the large square white-painted wood table that could easily seat eight, and motioning for her to sit down. His grandfather had built the table. He felt this weird urge to tell Claire that, but didn't. "Where did you find the placemats? I forgot I had these."

"I wasn't snooping," she said, sitting down, reaching out to finger one corner of the blue and white checked mat in front of her. "I was looking for spoons, and found them—top drawer of the island, in case you're wondering. They match the curtains, so I'm supposing someone made them? I can't imagine how you missed them."

"My mother, yes, and you'd be surprised what I miss in this place," he said, grabbing a can of ground coffee from a cabinet and loading the coffeemaker.

The clean and shiny coffeemaker, he noticed, with no brown drip stains on the base of it anymore. He'd been meaning to do something about that. Maybe even run some vinegar and water through it, which he was pretty sure he was supposed to do once in a while…probably more than once every two or three years.

"It's not like most men care about placemats," she said as he ladled soup into a bowl and carried it and a spoon over to the table. "I suppose having a son and a job keeps you busy. And it is a big house."

He found himself telling her about the house, its history, and the way it was passed from generation to generation. He even told her about the table.

She sat with her chin cupped in one hand, clearly fascinated, and let him talk. She didn't interrupt, didn't ask questions, and he heard himself saying things he'd never said aloud before.

Ending with, "My ex-wife hated it here. Said she felt smothered."

By now they were both on their second cup of coffee.

Claire lowered her mug and looked around the kitchen, and then nodded. "I can see that. A young bride, thrust into all of this tradition. She must have been afraid to touch anything, for fear she was messing with some treasured family heirloom."

"Not really. Sandy simply wasn't interested. Not her bag, she said. Too many things to manage, too much responsibility dragging her down. She liked to be able to pack and go on a moment's notice. A house...a house meant putting down roots, and she wasn't ready for that."

"But she had a child."

Nick stood up, carried his soup bowl over to the sink. "I told you. Sean was...he was a surprise. She tried, she really did, I'll give her that. She loved him, don't get me wrong. But in the end? In the end, Sandy had to be who she was, or at least who she wanted, wants, to be."

"I saw a photograph of her on Sean's night-stand, when I put him to bed. A very pretty woman. Full of life."

Nick knew the photograph well. It had been snapped on stage, the spotlights loving Sandy's slim form clad in brief black leather, backlighting her masses of blond curls like some sort of pagan halo around her beautiful, pouty-lipped face. God, how she came alive onstage. Whenever he looked at that photograph, Nick saw what he'd refused to see when he'd fallen in love with her. She might have once loved him, but she loved this other life more. She fed on it, couldn't survive without it. For Sandy, per-forming was a drug, and she was addicted.

"Nick?"

He turned away from the sink, realizing he'd been silent too long.

"I'm sorry. I was woolgathering there for a moment, I guess."

"It's all right. I've got to go. Office hours start at

nine. But I did want to ask how it went tonight if I could. Is the woman all settled at the shelter? And the children?"

He nodded and then walked with her, back toward the foyer. "For now, yes. God, she looked like hell, her right eye swollen shut like a boxer who'd gone one round too many with Muhammed Ali. The kids were better, acted like they were going to a party. I don't get it, Claire. I did the research, I wrote the articles. But I don't get it. What makes a man do things like that to a woman he professes to love?"

"I don't know. Insecurity? A need to control?" She picked up her purse and searched in it for her car keys, and then looked at him. "Did you ask any of them?"

Nick looked at her in some surprise. "Ask any of them? No. I was writing about these women, what happens to them. It never occurred to me to—damn it, Claire, it never occurred to me. I mean, they're animals, right? Jerks. Bullies. Subhuman. Who cares what they think?"

"I imagine somebody should, if there's to be any hope that they'll stop. They're people, too, Nick. Probably, to somebody, at least at times, they're very good people. Men with jobs, even meaningful careers. Possibly some of them are well-respected by those who don't know what goes on behind closed doors. So what makes them go off the rails, hit the women they love, abuse them physically or emotionally? There has to be a reason."

"The woman tonight? Her husband is a drunk."

"All right," Claire said, still being maddeningly reasonable. "But why is he a drunk? And you know, alcohol is the drug of choice for many unhappy people, a sort of self-medication. Why does he hit his wife or partner? Was his father a drunk? Did his father beat his wife in front of his son? Did the father beat him? Those who are abused often grow up to be abusers themselves."

"That's no excuse, Claire. Nothing you said is an excuse."

"Not an excuse, Nick. A reason." She spread her arms as if to encompass the foyer, the entire house. "This is your tradition. What if violence is that woman's husband's family tradition, and possibly hers as well? And is there a way to break that chain? No matter what the social status, the background, there must be something that connects all of these men…these abusers, these controllers. Aren't you at all curious to know what that is—or at least *ask?*"

Nick shook his head, a smile growing both inwardly and outwardly. "You're something else, Claire Ayers, do you know that? Now you've got me thinking I only did half my job with that series. What makes you so smart?"

She lowered her head, but he was fairly certain he saw something flicker in her eyes and then quickly disappear. "I was just spouting stupid things I learned in one of my psych classes in college, and I shouldn't have done it. I didn't say you only did half a job."

"I know. I'm the one who said that. And I'm right. According to everything I've read, and my discussions with the court psychologist, men like this woman's husband are at their most vulnerable, their most ashamed and contrite, right after one of their violent outbursts. Maybe I'll stop by the house tomorrow, see what comes of it."

Claire looked up at him sharply, her eyes wide. "And I certainly didn't mean for you to do anything like *that*. If you talk to any of these men, it should be in a controlled atmosphere. What if he's still violent?"

Before he could check himself, Nick reached out a hand and stroked the side of Claire's cheek. "It's all right. I know this PA who might patch me up and even make me some canned chicken and noodle soup."

"Not...funny," she said, and then sighed as she reached back into her purse and pulled out a business card. "Here. The office number is on there, and my cell. If you go see this man tomorrow, you have to call me afterwards and tell me what happened. And remember, if he swings, cover your mouth, or else you'll end up in the dentist's chair, and you don't want that."

And then, as he was chuckling at her verbal swipe at his phobia, she went up on her toes and kissed his cheek. "You're a nice man, Nick Barrington, with a nice son and a nice house. I think I'm glad I met you."

Nick stood in the doorway, watching as she made her way along the curved pathway, past the ground lights, beneath the wrought-iron trellis, and all the way to her car, which sat beside his in the driveway. He stayed in the doorway until her engine caught, her headlights went on and she backed up, turned and drove onto the street.

Once her taillights disappeared around the curve, he went inside, closed the door and leaned his back against the solid wood.

"Well," he said to the quiet house. "That was fairly pitiful, Romeo…"

He'd wanted to tell her that there had been something different about her tonight. Something with her eyes. They'd seemed…happier, somehow. But that would have been awkward, because it could mean that maybe she hadn't looked all that good the first time they'd met, talked.

Man, he really was out of practice, if he'd even forgotten how to pay a woman a compliment.

And not reacting to her kiss on his cheek? Not taking the moment and running with it? Kissing her back. Just letting her leave like that? Not asking where she lived, or making arrangements to pick her up Saturday night? Was there even going to *be* a Saturday night?

"Suave," he grumbled as he made his way back to the kitchen to rinse the dishes and put them in the dishwasher. "You're the new king of suave, that's what you are…"

* * *

Claire took a bath when she got home. She normally showered, her free time always seeming to be at a premium. But tonight a bath seemed in order. The warm water would relax her, perhaps cut through some of the caffeine from those two cups of coffee at Nick's house, and maybe even wash away the thoughts that had plagued her on the drive across town to her condo.

What on earth had prompted her to defend—yes, that was the only word for it—domestic abusers?

She knew the answer to that one. Lumping them all into the same pile would mean lumping Steven in with the man who had broken his wife's ribs tonight. Steven wasn't like that. He was a lawyer, highly respected. Financially solvent, active in the community. He'd never touched her in anger. Not once. He didn't fit the profile—but was there really a profile?

That's all she'd really been saying to Nick tonight, she believed. Abusers weren't one-size-fits-all.

And there were all different kinds and levels of abuse, her brother Derek had reminded her when she'd phoned him, told him about how Steven had been…God, stalking her. Mostly, Derek had told her what she wanted to hear: "Get out, now, sis. Come to Allentown. Vivien and I have plenty of room. And you know I've got a place for you in my practice. I've told you that before."

Admitting to failure. That had been so hard. Claire

recognized that she'd always been a chronic over-achiever, and failure didn't come easily to her. Derek had told her that she was blameless, that the fault was all squarely with Steven.

But was it? Was any relationship ever that black and white? Was there some reason Steven had been drawn to a woman who had made no secret about the fact that she planned to work at her chosen career after marriage, even after their children were born? Was there a reason she had been drawn to a man who wanted a stay-at-home wife, with him at the very center of her universe?

It had taken two years of weekly visits with Dr. Fallon before Claire had believed she at last under-stood that she was not responsible for Steven's actions, but only for her own. Actually that had taken one year. The second year, she and the psychologist had spent those weekly fifty minutes together learning all about Claire, and she'd emerged from the sessions more confident in who she was and more forgiving of herself for choosing to leave an un-tenable situation rather than try to somehow *fix* Steven, *fix* the unfixable marriage.

"If you want a fixer-upper, Claire, buy one of those neglected old pre–Civil War houses in down-town Allentown and have at it. Don't marry someone who needs fixing, because that they have to want to do on their own," Dr. Fallon had said during one of their final sessions.

And that had about summed it up for Claire.

Steven had married her hoping to "fix her up." Change her, mold her into what he wanted, what he needed. She hadn't seen the pitfalls because she'd been in love. She couldn't believe he didn't understand how much her career meant to her, and had closed her eyes and mind to the warning signs that had been there all along, before the marriage.

She could live with that now. They'd both made mistakes. Would he have eventually turned to physical violence? She'd never know, and never wanted to know.

What she did know now, at twenty-nine, was who she was. And that felt good.

Maybe it was time to stop treading water and take the new, aware Claire out for an airing of the romantic kind? Her unwanted baggage had been taken care of, which she considered important, because she didn't plan to make the same mistake twice. She had a great career she loved, her own condo, a nice car and money in the bank. She was happy in her own skin, content. She didn't *need* anybody.

A mental image of Nick Barrington's easy smile and laughing eyes danced across her brain.

They were so comfortable together. She'd never had conversations with Steven that touched on anything even close to the conversations she'd had with Nick in just their first two meetings. Silly, and then at times nearly profound. Refreshingly honest. She wasn't the type to play games, and neither was he.

"We're not lonely," she said out loud as she stepped out of the tub and wrapped herself in a fluffy bath towel. "Not either of us. But that doesn't mean we have to be alone."

She'd planned to stay home and try out the new highlighting hair color she'd seen advertised on television, put a couple of subtle blond streaks in her hair with the nifty "easy-to-use" applicator just in case Nick called and they really would be going to dinner and a movie the next night.

Because she'd be on call Saturday from six in the morning until four in the afternoon, Claire had Friday afternoon off, and she'd been five minutes of reading the directions and ten minutes of indecision as to whether or not she'd end up looking like a skunk away from opening the color bottle when the phone rang.

She grabbed it halfway through the second ring, checked the caller-ID, breathed out, "*Finally*," and hit the Talk button. "Hello, Nick. Should I be breaking out the First-Aid kit?"

His easy laugh was her answer, and she relaxed shoulder muscles she hadn't realized she'd been holding tense all day. "You should see the other guy."

"That's a joke, right?" she asked anxiously.

"And not a very good one, I'm guessing. Sorry. Seriously, Claire, I'm fine. And I think I may be in line for a merit badge of some kind, because I took your advice."

"*My* advice? I didn't tell you to go see that man today. That was all your idea, remember?"

"But it worked out."

Claire collapsed into a nearby chair. "Oh. Well, in that case, how brilliant was I?"

"Brilliant enough to make me realize that I was lumping the bad guys all together and writing them off, and not looking at them as, well, as people in their own right. Individuals. Not a good thing for a journalist to do, Claire. I'm supposed to stay objective. Anyway, this guy I got together with this morning? Sober, he's a really nice guy. Loves his wife, he says, loves his kids. He actually cried when he realized they'd left him."

"He might be a very good actor, you know," Claire felt it important to point out.

"Ah, ye of little faith. I didn't call until now because I was busy getting him in front of a judge I know and having him admitted to a treatment center that supposedly shows some good results. I think maybe it took coming home to an empty house to finally wake him up. He signed himself in for the full course, and the judge signed a separate order as well, so he can't change his mind. I don't know if that's the answer for him or his family, but I have to tell you, I feel a lot better. So, thank you."

Claire blinked rapidly several times, as her eyes had begun to sting with tears. "Ah, Nick."

"That's it? Ah, Nick? Ah, Nick what? Ah, Nick, what a nice thing to do? Ah, Nick, you're a stupid dreamer? Ah, Nick, you deserve a big fat kiss?"

She laughed. "No, that's it. Just, ah, Nick. Where are you now? Do you have a deadline or anything?"

"Nope, I filed my story this morning. I'm doing a three-parter on the new development of the old Bethlehem Steel property. It's more than just the new casino, you know. Anyway, I looked up your address in the phone book, and it turns out I'm not that far away from you. Sean and I are heading for a gym at a church on Fullerton Avenue, an away game for his basketball team, and I wondered if maybe you'd like to come along."

"Really?"

His voice was so low now she could barely hear him. "I know it's last-minute, but it was Sean's idea. I don't know what you did last night, but he seems to think you're not terrible."

"That's high praise, coming from a nine-year-old." Claire ran her hand through her hair, which she'd already broken out of its French twist in preparation for Operation Highlights. She was dressed in jeans and a ratty old T-shirt and not exactly ready for prime time. "How long until you get here?"

"I don't know. Ten minutes?"

"I'll be outside," she said, and then quickly hung up before she could change her mind. The T-shirt hit the floor before she made it to the bedroom closet, where she stood staring dumbly at the racks, as if she had nothing to wear.

Time. She was wasting time being a girl.

She grabbed a yellow cotton summer sweater

from the hanger and yanked it over her head, pulling her hair out from the neckline as she slipped her bare feet into a pair of rope sandals, and then headed for the bathroom.

On the way, she glanced at the clock on her beside table. How long ago had he called? Two minutes? That gave her five minutes, tops, before she should be on her way out the door and down to the parking lot.

Claire brushed her teeth, freshened her five-minute face with a two-minute touch-up, and then ran a brush through her hair and decided she'd just leave it down. Casual. She was going to go for casual. Not like she was fixing herself up because Nick was on his way.

"Liar, liar," she told her reflection in the mirror over the bathroom vanity. She thought her hair was one of her best features. Thick, and glossy, and down past her shoulders when she wasn't scraping it all back for work. Maybe she shouldn't think about highlights? She probably should have asked Marylou. Except, if Marylou thought she needed highlights, she probably would have already dragged her to some stylist named Francois, or something.

She'd just opened the main door of her building when she saw Nick's car pulling into the parking lot. She raised her hand and waved, and he pulled into the No Parking zone in front of the door.

"Perfect timing," he said as she slid into the front seat. "It's a talent. I like your hair like that."

"Thank you. I didn't have time to put it up."

He slid the gearshift into Reverse and backed out of the No Parking slot. "Like I said, perfect timing."

He was flirting with her. This was beyond being a nice guy. He was definitely flirting.

"Funny man," she said, and then quickly looked into the back seat, hoping she wasn't blushing. "Hi, Sean. I didn't know you played basketball. Thanks for inviting me along."

The boy looked up from his handheld computer game and nodded. "You said you like sports. Basketball is a sport."

"I know. I played on my high school team. I was a Forward, first string varsity. I wasn't good enough to play in college, though. Or tall enough."

"Tell Ms. Ayers what position you play, Sean."

The child looked a little rattled, as if he wasn't sure. "Um…you tell her, Dad."

"He's a guard. Not the shooting guard. But he's good for several steals during the course of the game."

"Scrappy, huh?" Claire smiled at Sean. "I look forward to watching you play."

"Uh-huh." Sean went back to his computer game, his ears turning a little red. He seemed embarrassed by her attention. Which was nice.

What wasn't nice was how involved with the game and the success of Sean in that game Claire became as she sat on the fifth row of the bleachers, her spirits rising and falling with the score.

By the time the fourth period was halfway over,

and the Wildcats had lost the lead for the tenth or twelfth time, she realized she was in danger of becoming a real basket case.

"Their number forty-three almost always drives to the right. If Sean only kept his eye on the boy's waist, he could tell which way he's moving before he even takes a step, and go right with him. I want to call instructions out to him, but I know I shouldn't," she told Nick, who was one of those good guys who clapped no matter which team scored a basket. Clearly the man had no feel for competition. "How can you be so calm?"

"I've been doing this since he turned six. Baseball, soccer, basketball and now karate tournaments. It's either learn to go with the flow or court ulcers, I guess." He lifted Sean's gym bag from the empty row of bleachers behind them and offered it to her. "Here. There's some crackers in here, and a couple of mozzarella sticks. You won't be tempted to yell if your mouth is full. I've tried it, when I'm tempted. It really works."

"Thanks, but I don't think so." She took the bag anyway and looked inside. Along with a jacket, the crackers and cheese, and an apple that looked to have passed its prime, there were also some action figures she almost recognized, and a plastic something-or-other that looked like it might be a futuristic car or plane or something.

It was kind of cute.

She pulled it out and held it, because if nothing

else, it kept her hands busy, and went back to watching the game.

With two minutes left, the Wildcats pulled ahead by seven points, and she began to relax.

"I think they've got it now," she told Nick, who looked at her, smiled and shook his head. "What?"

"Nothing. I like your enthusiasm, I guess."

"Yeah, well, if you're going to play, winning is better than losing. But I behaved, I'm good." As she spoke, she ran her thumbs back and forth on the underside of the toy. "Oh, there's some sort of button here," she said, lifting the toy and looking at the button. "These toys are something else, aren't they? I wonder what this button—*ohmigod.*"

It was one of those "That didn't just happen, did it?" moments that you relive several dozen times in varying reactions of horror, disbelief and hilarity.

A small yellow plastic disk about an inch across had just gone flying forward three rows, to hit a man in the back and then fall to the bleacher seat, unnoticed by the unintended victim, luckily.

"Excuse me a moment," Nick said, deadpan, as he stood up, nonchalantly climbed down the three rows of bleachers, picked up the yellow plastic disk, and returned to sit beside her once more. He took the toy from her now nerveless fingers, and reloaded it before slipping it back into the athletic bag. Then, with laughter in his marvelous green eyes, he sighed, shook his head and said mournfully, "We can't take you anywhere, can we?"

And that, Claire would remember days later, was probably when she began to fall in love with Nick Barrington.

## Chapter Four

"Okay, we've got that crisis settled, you've talked Skip into wearing a tux. Thank you, Nicky, I knew you could do it if anyone could. I can't believe how he fought me on this, when he was so adamant about having me wear a gown. Now, when were you going to tell me you're bringing a date to my wedding?"

It was Saturday afternoon and Sean was already at the bowling alley, beginning a long day of birthday partying with his best friend, Jacob, ending with the sleepover. When Barb had called, asking him to come over, Nick had readily agreed. It would help pass the time before he picked up Claire and they went to dinner.

Because, for reasons he didn't think he should explore too deeply, time had seemed to move at a snail's pace ever since he'd dropped her back at her condo yesterday after the game.

God, that was funny. Watching the Death Lasso go flying through the air toward another row of spectators (from the opposing team, which could have gotten nasty if the disk had hit the guy's head rather than its dying-swan lazy tap against his back). Hearing Claire's whispered *omigod*. But it was the horrified expression on her beautiful face that had been priceless; a real "grab your cell phone and take a picture for your Christmas cards" moment.

"Hmm?" Nick asked his cousin, still unable to hold back a smile every time he thought about Claire's reaction to his teasing, which was to bury her face against his shoulder as she tried to muffle her laughter.

It had been…*a moment*. Yes, that was it. One of those strange, unexpected, impossible to foretell or plan moments that could end up changing everything.

"I said, when were you going to tell me you're bringing a date to my wedding?" Barb repeated. "It's not like the reception isn't casual and there's just going to be tables, and no seating chart. But you could give a girl some warning. Aunt Beatrice already had someone lined up to bring as her guest, but now she's going to insist that Uncle Mick has to find some way out of his important business trip and come with her instead."

"Nice try, but I'm not buying it. Uncle Mick is an electrician, Barb, and the wedding is on a Saturday.

Two reasons the words *important business trip* and *Uncle Mick* don't go together. The words *Saturday afternoon baseball games on TV* and *Uncle Mick*? Now those two go together. Just out of idle curiosity, who was it?"

"Who was who?" Barb asked, twisting one of her dangling curls around her finger, a habit she'd had since childhood, whenever she was nervous.

"The woman, Barb. Who was the woman Aunt Beatrice was going to sic on me this time? I've seen quite the parade these last few years. The giggler. The Earth Mother. The gum-cracker. If we had more weddings and christenings in this family, one day I'd fully expect to see her dragging in some gal tossing flaming batons in the air as she whistles the *Battle Hymn of the Republic.*"

"Okay, okay, I get the point. Yes, she found somebody she thought you'd like. After all, Anita is my matron of honor, and you know she'll be sitting with Bill, not you. The two of them are inseparable."

"Anita is also about twelve months pregnant. You'd better just hope she makes it for another two weeks."

"She's *eight* months pregnant. Nobody is ever twelve months pregnant." Barb grinned. "But she does look it, doesn't she? She told me she's gained sixty pounds. She also says she doesn't know how. She said that to me when we had lunch last week, and as I watched her down her second double cheeseburger and a large order of fries. I don't want that to happen to me when Skip and I get pregnant.

Remember Sandy, when she carried Sean? She just had this cute little pot belly, and even then not until she was pretty far along."

Nick nodded his head, did his best to smile. Yes, he remembered when Sandy was pregnant with Sean. How she'd hated the changes pregnancy made to her body. Her band outfits were all leather, and leather didn't have the stretching ability of other materials, and revealed every body flaw. At one point he noticed that she'd pretty much stopped eating, and they'd had one hell of a fight.

But then she'd cried, said the wife of one of her band partners had told her that the baby just automatically fed off her body fat and there wouldn't be any problem. She was contrite. She was horrified that she might cause her own baby any harm. But she never did eat enough to allow Nick to relax, stop mentally counting her calories.

"You'll be a great mother, Barb. And Skip will make a great dad."

"I know. If we have girls, he'll be like putty in their hands, and if we have boys, he'll want them all to be offensive tackles, like he was." She leaned across the kitchen table and took Nick's hand in hers, squeezed it. "We both couldn't do any better than to watch you with Sean. You've been both mother and father to him, and he's a great kid. I'm…I'm sorry I mentioned Sandy. My timing was really off there, wasn't it? Now, tell me about your date for my wedding."

"First you tell me how you found out I have a date for the wedding."

Barb withdrew her hand and began playing with the straw in her glass of iced tea. "I went in for my fitting this morning. You know, at Second Chance Bridal? Chessie was there, and that woman you and I met the first day. Marylou Smith-Bitters. She's really nice. She—"

Nick held up one hand to stop her. "You don't have to say anything else. I get the picture. And you probably got chapter and verse about Claire."

"Yes, that's her name. Claire. Claire Ayers." Barb picked up her glass and spoke around the straw, her eyes twinkling with mischief. "Marylou's already got a gown picked out for her," she told him, and then took a long sip of iced tea. "She told Chessie to put it on hold for a month. Not that there's any pressure, Nicky, but just so you know the timeline."

"Okay, now that's not funny," Nick told her.

"No, I didn't think so, either. I thought it was *hilarious*. She makes Aunt Beatrice look like an amateur. Still, I can't wait to meet this Claire, as she sounds very nice. Has Sean met her yet? You don't want to do that too soon, you know."

"Too late for that advice, Barb. Claire and Sean have already met. He seems to like her. He asked me to invite her to his basketball game yesterday. You're saying that was a mistake?"

He didn't mention how he'd asked Claire to take Sean home on Thursday night, how she'd made him chicken and noodle soup and put him to bed. Sean, that was. She'd only made Nick the soup. And why did that thought come into his head?

But he shouldn't have asked her to take Sean home. When he looked back at that one, he saw the flaws on his own. He hadn't considered that Sean, virtually motherless these past six years, might so easily form an attachment to a female figure coming into his orbit.

"Well, if you're really back to dating—and it's about time—then I'd say don't make a habit out of bringing your dates around Sean, no. That sort of thing could confuse him."

"I'm not planning on installing a revolving door to my bedroom, Barb. It was one woman, and it was just a basketball game. Okay, and one other time. After class." He was about to explain more fully, reluctantly, when Barb interrupted to say that she already knew that he and Claire both taught classes at the community center, so that probably didn't count.

"We're keeping score?" he asked her, feeling like he'd just dodged a bullet.

"Not us, but I can't speak for Marylou Smith-Bitters. Oh, don't make that face. You know women can't help themselves when it comes to eligible single men. We have this *thing* about seeing them all happily settled down with the right woman."

"Which Sandy wasn't," Nick heard himself saying before he could edit his words. He rarely thought about Sandy anymore, often forgetting for months on end, and usually only remembering because Sean had done something wonderful and he thought the boy's mother should want to know about it. Which she probably wouldn't.

Except it had been different this week. Because this week had been different. Not that he was going to share that piece of not-so-great information with his cousin.

"I never said that, Nicky," Barb protested, and then sighed. "Oh, okay. No, she wasn't. You are over her, right? I mean, she really knocked you and everyone else for a loop when she took off like that. I can't say I ever really liked her, but nobody expected what she did. Leaving Sean like that, a baby just out of diapers? If I could have gotten my hands on her I would have wrung her neck for her. But you buckled down, and you're the best dad I know. I don't know if Claire is going to be the one, and that's none of my business. I'm just so glad you're seeing someone."

"I haven't been living in a cave for the last six years, Barb. I won't tell you Sandy didn't pretty much destroy me when she left, but I think that was more because of what she did to Sean than to me. We weren't happy, and both of us knew it. So, yes, I'm over Sandy, and have been for a long time. And I've dated my share of women."

His cousin tipped her head to one side, looking at him intently. "How many of them have you let within ten feet of your son?"

"None of them," Nick answered quietly. "Just Claire."

Barb's frown lifted into a smile. "Aha. I think I'm looking forward to meeting Claire."

Nick's smile was genuine. "I'll be sure to warn her."

Claire decided she'd hit the right note with the third outfit she'd pulled from the closet. Besides, she didn't really have a fourth; all her clothes seemed geared to the office and the chance they might end up with something wet and sticky on them, so they all needed to be wash and wear and Ironing Not Necessary.

But she liked the combination of slate-blue slacks and ivory silk sleeveless shell, plus the light, patterned zip-up collarless jacket her sister-in-law had given her on her last birthday. The materials were good, but the overall style remained simple, casual. The last thing she wanted to do was look as if she'd taken all sorts of pains to dress for the evening.

Even though she had.

She resisted pinning up her hair just because it was fast and easy, and bent herself in half so that the heavy mass of hair dropped toward the floor. Then she brushed through it again and again before standing up all at once, flipped her head back and watched in the bathroom mirror as her hair settled itself where it wanted to go. As usual, it "wanted" to tumble away from her forehead and temples and settle into soft waves that fell several inches beyond her shoulders.

She felt professional with her hair pinned back. She didn't want to feel professional tonight. She wanted to feel like a woman.

She might even need to; she hadn't felt much of anything for too long.

"Damn," she breathed as the doorbell rang. She gave a last quick look at her five-minute face, found her bone, open-toed heels as she passed through the bedroom, and managed to control her breathing by the time she opened the door to see Nick standing there.

"Hi," she said, shyness hitting her in a way that hadn't happened since she was in the third grade and her mother somehow wrangled a way to get her backstage at a New Kids On The Block concert, to meet the band. As she remembered the event, she'd stood there with her tongue stuck to the roof of her mouth, unable to make a single coherent sound. So *hi* was at least a step up.

"Hi, yourself," he said, smiling at her from the doorway. "You look…would it scare you off if I said you're beautiful?"

"I think I can handle it. Thank you. I *feel* like a woman who spent all day at the hospital and then rushed home so I could be on time for our…our date."

"In that case, I'm glad I made reservations at Emeril's. It sounds like you could use a relaxed dinner."

Claire snatched up her purse from the table beside the door and stepped outside, checking to be sure she had her key before closing the door. "Emeril's? As in *let's kick it up a notch*? I've watched him on TV. But he's opened a restaurant in the new casino, hasn't he?"

"His own steakhouse, yes. I've haven't been there yet, but I've heard good things, and figured tonight might be a good time to give it a try. Do you like steak?"

"I was raised in Chicago, Nick. You know, the Chicago stockyards? Asking me if I like steak is like asking someone raised in Maine if they like lobster."

"Good point. So your day was busy?" he asked as he held the car door open for her.

She gave him a quick recap of her day, and how thrilled she was to check out a set of quadruplets born two days earlier at the hospital, with all of them doing well in the NICU. "That's the Neonatal Intensive Care Unit," she told him. "But they're in great shape. Two of them haven't even needed oxygen. Tiny, though. The biggest just tops four pounds, with the second one close behind him."

"Sean was a little over seven pounds, and I was afraid to hold him. What in hell do you do with four babies at one time?"

"I'm not sure, but I'm guessing sleeping is pretty low on the list. We're seeing more and more multiples these days. I mean, they're not exactly commonplace, but this is the third set I've seen since I joined Derek's practice, so that averages out to one set a year. Other than the quads, my day was pretty much routine, signing out a few patients to go home. How was yours?"

He turned to look at her, his mouth opening, and

then he turned his attention back to the traffic on the bridge. "Let's see. I used dynamite to blast Sean out of bed for basketball practice at nine, brought him home, explained that everyone takes a shower after basketball, even if it isn't time for bed. That took a while. Got him to the bowling alley for the party after turning around and coming home only twice—once for his toothbrush, the second time for the present we forgot on the kitchen table. He gets his great organizational skills from me, obviously."

"Busy morning," Claire said, laughing. At the time, he must have been frustrated as hell, but in the telling, he'd made it all into a series of amusing father-and-son incidents. Sean was a lucky boy.

"The day got busier. After that, I grabbed a couple of hotdogs with my cousin's fiancé because I was ordered to talk him into wearing a tux even if he says he'll look like an overstuffed penguin in one—which he might. I mean, the man has a point, and a twenty-inch neck. Big boy, Skip is, you'll see him at the wedding. Not fat, just big, over six-six and built like an offensive tackle, which he was in college. And then I stopped in at my cousin's to report mission accomplished."

"She was pleased?"

"Yeah, she was. For someone who had to be talked into wearing a gown herself only a week ago, she's suddenly all gung-ho for the rest of the trappings. So now, since I'm best man, you get to see me looking like a penguin, too. Or also."

"I imagine you look very good in a tuxedo. I'm looking forward to it."

"I'm not. I haven't worn one since college, for some cotillion I got roped into attending my freshman year."

"And your wedding," Claire said.

"No, there was no wedding. We just went down to the courthouse and did it there." He sort of smiled, sniffed.

"What? What are you thinking about?"

"I was just thinking that the judge was dressed better than either one of us. I think we were both trying to tell each other it was just a piece of paper, a necessary legality, and really didn't mean anything. Which, as it turned out, it didn't."

"What's the line in that old song? Regrets, I have a few...?"

"Frank Sinatra, *My Way*. But, you know, Claire, I really don't. I've got my son, and he's worth everything to me. At twenty-two, I wouldn't say I was what's called a wild child, but I still wasn't thinking about actions and consequences, as I should have been. Sean's arrival made me wake up, grow up. Having a child to care for changes your entire life."

They'd stopped at a red light, and he turned to look at her again. "No, if somebody handed me one of those Reset buttons and I could go back, do things differently, I wouldn't change anything. It's what we experience, live through—survive—that makes us who we are, and I'm pretty content with who I am now. Plus, I can't picture my life without Sean in it."

And then he grinned at her, looking slightly sheepish. "And that's it for this episode of Profound Theater, I promise. I don't know why I tell you things I've never really said to anyone else, or maybe even thought about before, but I'll try to be better, I promise."

"Please don't stop on my account," Claire told him, touching his hand as it lay on the steering wheel before she could think better of the physical gesture. "I'm…I'm flattered that you'd trust me with such personal information."

When they got to the restaurant and had been seated, their orders taken and their wine poured, Claire finally said what she'd been rehearsing inside her head for the past ten minutes.

"You've been so open and honest with me, Nick. I feel as if I'd like to return the favor."

He immediately shook his head as he reached across the small square table and took her hand. "No, Claire, you don't have to do that. In fact, I don't want you to do that."

"But—"

"Let me finish. I don't want you to do that *tonight*. For some reason tonight seemed to be my time, but that doesn't mean it has to be your time."

She squeezed his hand, at the same time relaxing the last tense muscles in her body. "Thank you."

After that, their conversation ranged across a half dozen subjects. They agreed on most of the topics, only parting ways when it came to the proper preparation of filet mignon. Claire liked hers medium-well, but Nick preferred his rare, very rare. Cool-in-the-center rare.

"Next time, Dracula, why don't you just tell them to march a cow through here and you can take a bite out of it," she teased him with that old joke, looking with some distaste at the now congealing juices on his otherwise empty plate. Even his vegetables were all gone, which was more than she could say for her own plate.

"You're just saying that because you can't stand the sight of blood."

"I'm a PA, Nick. I'd have chosen another profession if I couldn't stand the sight of blood. And that's not blood on your plate. It's juice. Sort of. I hope."

"You know, until a few years ago, I'd never heard of a physician assistant. What made you choose to become one?"

She sat back so that one server could remove their dishes and another hand them the dessert menu. A quick look at the choices had her regretting that she felt much too full for anything more than a cup of coffee.

"We could split one," Nick offered, at that moment looking more like his son than he probably knew, so that she agreed, inwardly wondering if she could eat another bite. But she could pretend, leaving more for him.

"I'm full, too, but I don't think I've ever turned down dessert. Especially one that promises to have that much chocolate in it. Now, back to why you became a PA."

Pushing back the thought that, in some countries, chocolate was considered an aphrodisiac, Claire launched into her explanation.

"Derek, my brother, went to med school, and I thought about doing the same, but decided on nursing instead. Halfway through, it occurred to me that I didn't want nursing, either, but something sort of in between. It's a rapidly growing field, and I couldn't be happier. Did you always plan to be a journalist?"

Nick nodded, his mouth full of chocolate cake. His face took on an expression of delight before he swallowed, smiled and said, "The man doesn't lie, that's definitely chocolate. Go on, try a bite."

"I'd hate to deprive you," she told him, but then dipped her fork into the confection sitting between them. "Oh," she said moments later, guiding her fork back to the plate for another taste. "That's indecent."

"Bordering on X-rated, yes. We each should have ordered one."

"Never! We'll always just have to share."

The moment the words were out of her mouth she wanted to kick herself. But Nick only smiled, and agreed with her.

She might be digging into a slice of chocolate cake, but suddenly she felt as if she were digging a hole straight into potential trouble. She was liking this man much too much, and definitely much too fast.

"To answer your question," Nick said, thankfully dropping the subject of future shared desserts, "do you remember Watergate?"

"The Washington, D.C., hotel, or the scandal?"

"Actually, the movie about the scandal. And the book. All the books about the marvels of investigative journalism. My dad's a political junkie and pointed me toward the first book while I was still in high school. I took it from there. I was going to be just like Woodward and Bernstein."

Claire nodded. "The journalists. I remember hearing the names somewhere. But that was a long time ago."

"Maybe too long ago, I agree. A lot of things have changed since then, most especially newspaper journalism. You're looking at one of a dying breed, Claire. Which is why I'm now also writing a twice-weekly online column for a site a few of us have going. We get more readers there in one day than the entire weekly circulation of the *Chronicle*, with the advantage of being global, not local. If print newspaper circulation keeps going down, soon people will have to find other ways to line their birdcages and wrap up yesterday's fish bones."

"I feel so responsible," Claire told him. "I'm one of those people who gets most of my news from TV and the Internet. I still have the *Chronicle* delivered every morning, but that's more out of habit than anything else. Often I don't get past the front-page headlines."

He'd paid their bill and they were walking out of the restaurant, which led them straight onto the casino floor. "I forgive you. Progress happens, that's all. You either go with it or get left behind. For instance, look over there."

She looked where he was pointing, and her jaw dropped. "What on earth is that?"

She saw two rows of what looked to be kiosks, each one containing a huge video screen and fronted by a semi-circle sort of bar with attached and, at the moment, empty chairs. On the screen was the image of a woman standing in front of a green-topped table. She seemed to be looking around the large casino floor, appearing wistful and slightly bored. Not to mention beautiful and artificially enhanced.

"That, Claire, is the twenty-first century version of a blackjack table. She smiles as she takes your money, talks to you, and you don't even have to tip her when you get up to leave. It's when I think about the newspaper business, and things like that virtual dealer doing the job real people used to do, that I realize maybe I'm a bit of a Luddite."

"Really? If you feel yourself being overcome by some urge to go over there and smash the machines, let me know."

"You'll restrain me?" Nick asked her, grinning.

"Nope. I'll head for the door and pretend I never saw you before in my life. I'm no fool."

He laughed and slipped his arm around her waist, which felt nice. "Come on, let's get out of here. Unless you want to gamble? We probably missed the last show anyway. I didn't realize we'd talked so much over dinner."

Claire looked at the rows and rows of slot machines and the crowds of people eager to try their luck. "Just getting up every day is enough of a gamble for me, I think. Maybe we could go somewhere else?"

He turned her toward the valet parking desk, bending close so that he could almost whisper his next words into her ear. "We could always go back to my house, Ms. Ayers, and I could show you my etchings."

"Now *that's* gambling," she told him as her heart performed a flip that would probably score at least a seven-point-three at the Olympic games.

"Life's a gamble, Claire," he told her, suddenly serious. "I guess it all comes down to whether or not we're willing to take a risk. If I'm going too fast for you, just let me know."

She bit her bottom lip as she lowered her gaze to the tiled floor for a moment, drew in a breath and let it out slowly. "No," she said, looking up at him, refusing to blink. "I don't think you are."

## Chapter Five

"I keep telling myself we're both adults."

Nick and Claire were standing face-to-face in his bedroom, moonlight streaming in through the nearly floor-to-ceiling small-paned windows that faced the rear of the house. They were holding hands, and looking at each other in the soft, intimate darkness.

"And how's that working out for you?" she asked him, knowing she sounded slightly breathless.

His smile pretty much wiped away the rest of her nervousness. "I guess you could say, so far, so good."

They'd shared their first kiss as they waited for the valet to bring his car. It was a short kiss, as they were fairly public. But it wasn't just perfunctory.

She'd tasted him in that kiss, and his lips had been warm, encouraging rather than insistent.

She'd liked that.

He held her hand when he could during the drive, occasionally raising it to his mouth. Keeping contact. Holding the mood. Melting her in ways she only vaguely remembered, or perhaps had never experienced before Nick touched her.

The night was so quiet, the world hushed, the mood expectant.

Nick leaned in, caught her mouth with his own. Once. Twice. A third time. Until she followed him as he retreated, took the initiative.

"You taste good," he told her. "Like chocolate."

She tipped her head, began nuzzling at the side of his neck. It was like coming home. She felt warm, safe, and yet delighted to be there. "Considering how you enjoyed the cake, I'll take that as a compliment."

He let go of her hands to slide his arms around her waist, and she raised hers to encircle his shoulders. "If there was music, we could be dancing."

"I thought we were."

His laugh was low, easy. "True. How about we sit this next one out?" Taking her hand, he led her over to the bed, turned her so that her back was to it. "I want you so much."

He was so honest, not that he could hide the intensity of his expression, or the physical evidence of his arousal as he pressed lightly against her. She returned the pressure with her hips, probably the oldest signal in the world, offering herself to him.

They were still dancing, but the melody had changed. There were no more bantering, no more teasing lyrics. Now it was the evocative throb of the saxophone that ran through her veins; provocative, blatantly sexual.

She made the first move, stripping off her jacket, lifting the silk shell up and over her head, her hair resettling itself around her shoulders.

Nick didn't reach for her bare midriff, move to cup her breasts.

No. He slid his hands into her hair, threading his fingers into the thick waves as he pulled her closer, slanted his mouth against hers. Now his kiss was deeper, more intimate, mimicking the physical union that was as anticipated as it was inevitable.

*Three years. Three years.* Toward the end, she and Steven hadn't had much left between them except the sex, and she'd been celibate since then by both choice and inclination.

Now she wanted. She felt the need. And, to be here with Nick, she had to believe her reawakened sexual appetite wasn't the only reason.

She knew it wasn't. She wasn't that shallow, and Nick was so much more than an opportunity for release. She craved his touch, yes. But *his* touch, his alone. If she believed that physical desire was enough she'd not have learned anything at all in the last three years, not about life, and not about herself.

Nick had discarded his sport coat in the living

room, and now, somehow, his tie was hanging around Claire's neck as he stripped off his dress shirt. And he'd done it all without ever really leaving her, their mouths clinging for endless moments, his touch never really gone from her as he'd found the front catch on her bra, sighed into her mouth as her breasts were released and then cupped by his large hands.

Claire reached for his belt, her hands steady. There was no reason to fumble, no nervousness or hesitation. They needed to be closer, she and Nick, and she took the next logical step.

As did he.

And all without undo haste. All accomplished amid sweet kisses and increasingly intimate caresses. They each explored new territory, learning the landscape of one another until they were both naked in the moonlight.

"I never knew anyone could be so beautiful," Nick whispered as he picked her up, laid her down on crisp white sheets that were cool against her skin. "Or that I could want someone so much."

She held up her arms, beckoning him to join her on the bed. "You don't have to say that, Nick. I'm here with you because I want to be here with you."

He lay down beside her, pulling her into his arms. "And I'm smart enough not to ask you why that is. I'm just going to be glad you are."


Nick awoke and turned his head to look at the bedside clock. It was after three. They'd been asleep only two hours, so what had wakened him?

But as he turned his head once more, to look at the woman who slept in the crook of his arm, he closed his eyes against the full moon and the light that shone straight through the windows and into his face. He always closed the drapes when the moon was full, having quickly learned that moonlight can at times be as intrusive as sunlight.

Except that tonight he blessed the light, for it fell on Claire, too. On her magnificent caramel hair as it tumbled around her face. On one slim white shoulder, the sweet dip and curve of her waist and hip.

She looked so serene in sleep. A woman. In her mind, in her heart, in her decisions. *I'm here with you because I want to be here with you.*

Her words had been humbling. He'd been humbled. And his passion for her, his desire, his need for her, had doubled, and then redoubled again.

There'd been no further reason for speech. They needed to feel, both of them. Those words may have been unspoken, but they both knew what the other needed. He knew his own reasons, but not hers. But that didn't matter. She'd tell him when she felt able, and he'd wait until then.

He began smoothing back her hair from her cheek, not in order to wake her, but because he couldn't resist touching her. Her hair was so thick, warm, almost alive. He hoped she'd wear it down more often. The professional Claire was beautiful, yes. But the Claire now sleeping in his arms was so much more than beautiful. She was also vulnerable, and trusting, and, at least for the moment, his.

She opened her eyes, her lids still heavy with sleep, and then looked up at him. Smiled a sleepy smile. "Hi."

"Hi, yourself," he said, gazing down at her, feeling himself once more drowning in her soft brown eyes.

*Occhi molli di un Madonna.* The soft eyes of a Madonna.

"Is your arm asleep?" she asked him, pushing herself up and away from him, dragging the sheet along with her to cover her breasts as she sat looking at him. "You should have pushed me off."

"What, and give up the view?"

"Very funny." Claire let the sheet drop as she finger-combed her hair away from her face, utterly uncaring of her nakedness. Again, he felt a surge of feeling that came immediately after a thought he'd had before: she trusted him. He hadn't known such a thing would matter so much to him, but it did.

"I probably look like Medusa, except for the snakes, I mean. This is more like a rat's nest. I really should get it cut. It would be much more practical."

"I refuse to kneel at your feet, sobbing 'please don't, please don't.' But feel free to imagine the scene," Nick told her, lazily trailing his fingertips up and down her long, smooth thigh. "Are you hungry? Thirsty? Horny?"

She blinked at him, and then laughed, a sound he could happily listen to for the rest of his life, he realized. "How about all of the above?"

"Ah, I like that answer." He got out of bed, pulled on his dress slacks sans belt, and tossed his dress shirt to her. "If madame would care to join me in the kitchen?"

"Madame would, thank you."

He waited until she'd buttoned the shirt, which had never looked half so good on him, and then waited until she was walking, barefoot, down the hall, taking a moment to enjoy the view once more before he followed her.

She lowered bread into the four-slice toaster as he poured orange juice into two glasses and pulled butter and grape jelly from the refrigerator. They moved around the kitchen as if they'd been working together for years, not bothering to turn on the over-head lights, as the under-the-counter lights, along with the moonlight shining through the bay window behind the table, were enough.

Nick thought his kitchen had never looked better, because Claire was in it.

He stood behind her as she buttered the toast, sliding his hands beneath the long tails of his shirt that reached halfway down her thighs, not stopping until he could spread his hands against her flat stomach and midriff. "Ticklish?" he asked as he lightly licked at the side of her neck.

"Don't you just wish," she said, and then shivered. "Is this your way of telling me you aren't hungry?"

"I thought I was telling you just the opposite," he whispered. And then, to prove his point, he began nibbling at her earlobe. "Umm, I wonder if you'd taste even better with jelly."

She turned in his arms, nearly shoving a slice of toast in his face. "Nibble this—and control yourself. Because I really am hungry."

"And I'm pitiful. Sorry," he said, taking the toast as he pulled out a chair at the table for her. "Here. Sit, eat."

"In a minute. I want to get something from my purse."

He watched her pad out of the kitchen, heading once more toward the bedroom. He would have been more curious if he didn't enjoy watching those long legs so much.

She was back quickly, and took the chair he'd offered. "Now we'll eat. And talk."

He sat down and looked at her in surprise. "Talk? All right. What do you want to talk about?"

"Our china pattern," she said, her brown eyes twinkling. She laughed, shaking her head. "Oh, you should have seen yourself, Nick. Anyone would think I'd just announced that I'm actually an alien."

"From some other country…or solar system?"

"Don't worry, earthling, I come in peace," she said, and then took another bite of toast, the tip of her tongue snaking out quickly to snare a bit of jelly that clung to her bottom lip.

Which was the sexiest move he'd ever seen, and he's seen his share of them.

"Just don't make jokes like that in front of Marylou, or my Aunt Beatrice, okay, or they'll be renting a hall."

She put down the toast she'd been eating so eagerly, and looked him fully in the eye. "I already had that. The hall, I mean. The bridal registry, the shower, the white gown and the bridesmaids, the church wedding and the reception complete with rubber chicken and tasteless wedding cake."

"And the groom," Nick added quietly. "What happened?"

He asked this already sensing that her answer wasn't going to be that she'd stashed him somewhere and she was still married.

"We divorced. About three years ago, which is a lot longer than we were married. I should have told you sooner."

"No, not really. I don't think either of us asked for a resume. But I'm glad you're telling me."

"Yes, I guess I am, too. The marriage was a mistake, right from the beginning. We both...we each thought we were marrying someone else."

"Excuse me?"

She smiled, and there was that soft sadness in her eyes again, a regret she'd learned to live with, he supposed. "I thought Steven understood and supported my career, and he thought I'd forget my career and make him not just the center of my world, but my entire world. Never believe loving someone will make him or her change, or make it possible for you to change the person. Because it doesn't work."

Nick had a quick mental flash of Sandy dressed in her stage clothes and on her way out the door, arguing with him that he could take Sean to the pediatrician himself if he thought the kid was sick, that it didn't take two parents to sit bored to tears in a waiting room full of snotty, screaming kids.

Marriage hadn't changed Sandy. Parenthood hadn't changed her.

But both had changed him.

"I guess it depends upon the person," he said quietly.

"Yes, I guess it does. That's called growth. I like to tell myself that I tried as hard as I could, but I'll never know that, will I? Six months isn't much of an effort."

"So you went your separate ways. Was the divorce amicable?" He tried to tell himself that it was only the journalist in him, asking logical, follow-up questions. But that would be a lie.

Claire picked up their empty plates and carried them over to the sink. "No," she said, her back to him. "Not really."

He took the juice glasses to the sink, and stopped Claire as she was about to rinse everything and put it in the dishwasher. He took her hand in his. "Come on, let's sit down again. The dishes can wait. Around here, they're used to it."

She smiled at his small joke, and allowed him to lead her back to the table. He sat down and pulled her into his lap.

"I'm sorry," Claire said, blinking. "I just need to always remember that it takes two to make a marriage, and two to make a divorce. If I don't acknowledge my own mistakes, then I would be destined to make the same mistakes again."

Nick had an arm around her, to keep her steady on his lap. He took hold of one of her hands as they lay in her lap, hoping to reassure her as well as to stop her from wringing them, something he doubted she realized she was doing.

"I agree there, Claire. We may fall in love with the dream, but we wake with the reality. You know what happened with Sandy and me. I think we were already about done with the dream when she realized she was pregnant."

"I can't even say that. We were about three weeks from the wedding when Steven's teasing about when I was going to quit my job finally penetrated my brain for what it really was—his insecurity, even jealousy. But, as I said, I thought he'd be all right with it. And, yes, there were my parents, and the rented hall, and the wedding cake already ordered, and the presents coming in…"

"You thought it was too late to call it off."

"Derek said I should, but I just couldn't do it. That was my mistake, and one I really have learned to live with. After that, when Steven started…"

Facts, things he already knew, started numbering themselves in his brain. She'd left Chicago and come to Allentown, to her brother. Who hadn't liked Steven, obviously. She'd taken back her maiden name. She'd shown an intense, clearly informed interest in his articles on domestic violence. She damn near defended the men who physically or mentally abused their wives, telling him that there were always reasons, always problems on both sides of the relationship. She'd said much the same just now.

He totaled up the numbers, and came up with an answer that gave him a cold, unsettling feeling in his belly.

"When Steven started what, Claire? Did…did he hit you?"

She shook her head, her hair falling forward, obscuring most of her face. "No, it never got that far. After the wedding, when we got back from the honeymoon, the teasing about my job went away, and the complaints started. He worked hard, he expected to come home to a hot meal and a wife who was happy to see him. He earned enough for the two of us. More than enough, and he did. Steven's a lawyer," she told Nick, pushing back her hair and turning to look at him. "I'll say this for the man, he knew how to construct an argument and verbally take apart his opponent. Top of his class."

"Did he drink?"

Finally, she smiled. And her eyes were dry. "You're doing it again, Nick. Trying to lump them all together. No, Steven didn't get drunk and abusive. He's highly educated, a good friend and very well liked. He doesn't fit the mold because there is no mold. We can never presume to know what goes on behind the closed doors in any marriage."

"No, I suppose not. But you argued."

"*Steven* argued. *I* apologized. I'm sorry I got stuck

at the office when an emergency backed up appointments. I'm sorry I have to go to bed so early tonight, but I've got a chance to observe in the OR tomorrow. I'm sorry dinner was late. I'm sorry, I'm sorry, I'm sorry. Until I wasn't sorry anymore."

"Something happened," Nick said, nodding his head. "What?"

"Steven went into cross-examination mode, I guess you'd call it. Where was I? What was I doing? When would I leave, and where would I be going next? Would there be men there? Phone calls, all day long, checking up on me. If I was going to stop at the grocery store on the way home, how long would that take, because it shouldn't take more than twenty minutes longer than my usual commute. God forbid there was a line at the express checkout, because then I'd be late, and the questions would start all over again—did I see anyone, talk to anyone? Who? It got so that I was a nervous wreck, silently cursing people who didn't unload their carts fast enough or who'd brought sixteen items into the ten-item limit line. A nightly Inquisition he stopped even pretending was just a natural interest in my day. It became obsessive. I couldn't breathe."

Nick began rubbing his thumb over the back of her hand. "His problem, Claire, not yours. His insecurities. It wasn't your career. It was him."

"I know that now," she told him. "I suggested counseling, but Steven wouldn't agree. And then I looked in the rearview mirror one day, and saw his car. He was following me. Tailing me, as if I were some criminal."

"Cripes. You can't blame yourself for that, Claire."

"I know. It took me a while, but I know. I called Derek, he said leave everything, get on a plane, come to him. Steven may never have raised a hand to me, or even his voice, but I understand women— people—like the woman you helped get to a shelter. When it's time to go, it's time to go. Things don't matter. Clothes, furniture, the house in you live in. Nothing matters but getting out, saving yourself."

"Did he contest the divorce?"

Finally, she smiled. "You haven't met Derek, have you? My big brother is so gentle with a newborn, so funny and reassuring with all of his young patients. But you mentioned your cousin's fiancé. Skip? I have a feeling Derek could give him an argument on which of them looks more like a stuffed penguin in a tux. Derek went to school in London and was captain of the rugby team, if that gives you more of an idea. He flew to Chicago the day after I arrived in Allentown, to settle things, he said. I don't know what happened, and I don't want to know, but Steven agreed to the divorce. Oh, and he's getting married again. He called me to tell me. I can only hope he also learned from his mistakes."

She rested her cheek against Nick's bare chest. "And that's my story, chapter and verse. I...I just thought you should know."

"Thank you for telling me. And I think I'm glad I

don't have to fly to Chicago and beat up your ex. I guess it wouldn't be good to send your brother flowers, huh?"

She lifted her head, smiled up into his face. "Men. You all want to punch something, as if that's the answer to every problem. Why is that?"

"It's our base male animal instincts, I suppose. I've other base male animal instincts, you know. Can you guess which one I'm having now? Or are you just going to keep moving around on my lap like that until my eyes roll up in my head?"

"Oh, you poor baby," she said. "You mean when I move like this? Or…like this? Oh, gosh, Nick, now my shirt is riding up, and I'm not wearing any—"

He growled low in his throat as he swooped down at her, plundered her mouth with an assurance that she would welcome his intensity, his passion.

They'd played the game when they'd first come together, the game of do you like when I do this, what happens when I do that? They'd been slow, exploratory, learning each other.

And they'd learned that they were good together. Very, very good together.

When she touched him now, her touch was sure, certain and marvelously blatant. She unzipped his slacks and reached inside, taking him in her hand, moaning low in her throat as she gauged his arousal, obviously approved.

She pushed his slacks down lower on his hips, and then did something he hadn't expected. Fantasized about, he supposed, but never before experienced.

She stood, looked down at his arousal, and then knelt in front of him. She reached into the pocket of his shirt…and pulled out a foil wrapped package.

"You—"

"I'm a terrible person, yes. And I could have been horribly wrong about what might happen between us tonight, or at least soon. But I'm also an optimist, I guess. Do you mind?"

Nick shook his head. "I'm a base male animal, Claire. I never said I was an idiot. Here, let me have that."

"No," she said, kneeling in front of him once more. "It can't be much different than putting on latex exam gloves."

"Now, that's romantic," he teased, and then he did his best to withhold a gasp as he watched her. "Come here," he all but begged. "Please."

She straddled him, slowly lowered herself over him. Taking him in. All the way in.

After that, Nick didn't remember much of anything, although the experience had definitely blown all of his fantasies out of the water…

## *Chapter Six*

Nick took Claire home before noon Sunday, closing the door on what had been their short, too short, weekend together. They'd talked about picking Sean up from his sleepover together, and they'd both decided it wasn't a good idea.

Neither of them said exactly why it wasn't a good idea.

Nick said he had to go grocery shopping, and then maybe visit Barb so that she could convince Sean that he wasn't too old to be a ring bearer, and then break the news that this honor brought with it the necessity of being measured for a tuxedo.

Claire told him that she had some medical reading to catch up on, as she had to take continuing classes to stay current, and that Sunday was her only day to clean the condo and do laundry.

Neither of them said that it was too soon to bring Sean into their relationship. If that's what they had now. A relationship.

Nick thought they might. He hoped they might.

But then there was Steven, the ex. He'd held on too tightly, tried to take over Claire's world. Nick didn't think it would be a good move on his part for him to crowd her too much, make any assumptions.

They were already moving pretty fast. Granted, they were adults, and they'd each made a choice. But a choice for a weekend and a choice for more than that were two different things. Involving Sean in something that might not last would be too confusing for a nine-year-old. Especially since he'd taken such an instant liking to Claire.

And there was that other thing. The thing he'd have to deal with if it became necessary. But he hadn't heard any more on the subject for two weeks, so he was pretty much ready to write it off as just another of Sandy's "moments." She'd probably forgotten she'd even written to him.

Please God.

Nick reached for his phone about ten times on Monday before he finally decided that to call Claire had to be better than to not call her. Their weekend had been too intense to not call her, to just wait for class on Tuesday night.

The intimacies they'd shared, both physical and

in how they'd talked of their lives? There needed to be some sort of bridge between that and seeing her in the hallway, saying a casual *hi, how are you* before heading for their own classrooms.

His call went to voicemail, something that, for all his careful planning, he hadn't anticipated.

"Claire, hi," he said, knowing modern technology would still leave his electronic footprint on her cell phone, even if he just hung up. "It's, uh, me. Nick. I hope you had a good day yesterday. I thought I'd tell you Barb worked her magic with Sean, and he's agreed to wear the tux. I only owe him three superhero figures and a trip to see that new 3-D movie on Saturday. Well, okay, I can see Fred waving to me from across the newsroom, so I've got to go. Maybe we can have some pizza together in the cafeteria after class tomorrow? My treat. Bye."

He pressed the End button and mastered the urge to beat his own cell phone against his forehead. He'd handled that about as smoothly as he had Sean's question of a few months ago: "Dad? Where do babies come from?"

He picked up his laptop and went out to the patio to write his next article for the blog. That was the one beauty of cell phones. People could lie about where they were. Say they were in church, or on their way someplace important, or in the newsroom, when they were really sitting behind a hot fudge sundae at the mall, or in front of a slot machine…or pacing the floor at home, wasting time that moved much too slowly, thinking about a girl with caramel hair and soft Madonna eyes.

When the phone rang about an hour later, he nearly knocked the laptop to the flagstone as he grabbed at it. He flipped it open, looked at the number, and felt his blood freeze in his veins.

"Nick Barrington here," he said with as much coolness and detachment as he could manage.

"You didn't write me back. Or call me, and I put the number in my letter. Did you think I'd forget?"

"Oh," he said, holding the phone in a death grip as he rubbed at his temples. "Hi, Sandy."

His ex-wife gave a short laugh, heavy with sarcasm. "Right. Like you didn't check your caller ID and know it was me."

"I'm sorry. I was working, and my mind wasn't really on—"

"Never mind, Nick. I don't blame you. As blasts from the past go, this one must be a real bummer for you. But you did get my letter, didn't you?"

He hit Save and closed the laptop, placing it on the wrought iron table beside the chaise. "Yes, I got it. Look, Sandy—"

"Cassandra."

"Excuse me?" he said, his eyebrows lifting, even though she couldn't see his expression. A good thing, too, and the day everyone routinely could see everyone else at the other end of the phone was the day he'd long for two tin cans and a string.

"I'm using my more formal name now."

"Your *formal name* is Sandra," he pointed out, and then mentally kicked himself. With Sandy, it was smarter to just go along, not argue.

"Cassandra is a form of Sandra."

Maybe. Who knew. He did retain enough Greek mythology from college, though, to remember that Cassandra was the daughter of some king of Troy or somewhere, and that she prophesied disasters. Sandy, Cassandra, disaster. They could be synonyms. Maybe he'd better stop stalling and just listen.

"All right, Cassandra. Why are you calling?"

"Is Sean there? Can I talk to him?"

"It's September, Sand—Cassandra. He's in school."

"Oh. Right." She laughed, rather nervously. "I should know that, shouldn't I? I mean, I *am* his mother."

"You gave birth to him, yes," Nick couldn't resist saying. "Look, Sandy, what do you want?"

"What do you think I want? I thought my letter was very clear. I want to see my son."

"Why?" *And why now? Of all the times you had to choose from in the last six years, why now, damn it!*

"Since when do I need a reason to see my own child, Nick?"

Calm. He had to stay calm. Think rationally.

The hell he did!

"Let's think this through, all right? You haven't been a part of his life in a long time. I need to know what you're thinking, Sandy—Cassandra. Is this going to be a one-time thing? Is your band going to be performing in Philly or something, and you thought it might be fun to drop by, see the kid? And then what? Then you disappear again for another six years? Because I can't let you do that, I really can't."

"The band broke up."

She'd spoken quietly, and then he heard her shaky intake of breath.

Cripes, was she crying?

"The band broke up? Is that what you said?"

"Sort of. Richie brought in another female singer. Without so much as asking me. And he gave her half my songs. I think…I think he's banging her. He says he's not, but I don't believe him."

Just what Nick needed, tales of Sandy's love life. "So then the band broke up? Sort of?"

"Not…not really. I left. I told him, lose the skank or I'm gone."

"Lovely language, Sandy. I remember when you were an English major."

"Sorry. I'm just so upset. Am I too old, Nick? Is thirty too old? Is that why he brought her in? I've still got my looks. And my voice is just getting better and better. I'm just coming into my prime. I thought…I thought Richie loved me. I thought we *had* something, you know? Even a cosmic connection."

Nick let her ramble on a while longer, until she'd gotten her tears under control, and then tried again.

"I don't know what to say to you, Sandy, except that I'm sorry things ended up not working between you and Richie. I'm sure you're feeling alone, lonely. But you can't drag Sean into this, you just can't. He's not a consolation prize."

He heard a beep on his end of the phone, wondered if it was Claire, calling him back. But there was nothing he could do about it at the moment. He had to convince Sandy to stay where the hell she was.

"Where are you, Sandy?" he asked her.

"Vegas. Well, almost Vegas. Laughlin. We're almost there, Nick. After all these years, we're almost there. Richie says that why he brought Crystal in. That we needed two female singers to get a gig in one of the casinos in Vegas. Not the Strip, not yet. But one of the smaller ones, just to start, you know. But I'm not buying that one. He wants me gone. I gave up everything for him, and this is what he does to me. I gave up my *son.*"

That hadn't been apparent at first, Sandy's romantic involvement with Richie. She hadn't flaunted it, hadn't thrown Richie Coughlin's name in his face as she walked away from their marriage. It had been all about her, about how she needed to have some space, devote all her time to her career, take her shot while she was still young enough to do so, or else she'd regret it forever.

Looking back on those days, Nick still couldn't believe how naïve he'd been. Or maybe he just hadn't cared enough anymore to think much about why Sandy had gone. She hadn't tried to take Sean with her, hadn't pushed for custody. That had been enough for him.

He got to his feet, as if standing up would somehow put him more in control. "I can't let you do this, Sandy."

She was crying again. "Do what?"

"Use Sean as an excuse. Come here because you and your lover broke up and you're looking for a place to land. I won't allow it."

"You won't *allow* it?" The tears were gone now, and her voice was hard, cold. "You sit there in that stuffy old house with your piles of family money and your do-gooder attitude—I've read the stuff you write online, Nick—and you think *you* can tell *me* what I can and can't do? He's my son, too, Nick Barrington, and don't you forget it! You know what? Let's see what a *lawyer* says, okay?"

She cut the connection, and Nick was left standing in the warm September sun, holding a dead phone to his ear until he finally closed it, just to have it ring again.

He opened it without looking at the number printout. "Sandy, I'm glad you called me back. Look, can't we discuss this as rational a—"

"Nick? It's me, Claire."

He squeezed his eyes shut as he grimaced, trying to change gears.

"Claire, I'm sorry. I was just on the phone with—well, you know who was on the phone. My ex."

"Let me take a wild stab at this—it wasn't a pleasant conversation. If you want to call her, I can get off the line."

"No," he said, subsiding onto the end of the chaise. "I don't want to call her back. Truthfully, I'd like to pretend the conversation never happened. I tried to call you earlier. I thought maybe you were on your lunch break."

"Lunch break? I don't think I understand the term," she said, laugher in her voice. "I mean, officially, we close the office for an hour each noon, but that mostly means we grab sandwiches at our desks as we catch up on morning calls to parents, other physicians' offices, the hospitals. If it weren't for pharmaceutical reps bringing in lunches for us fairly often, we might all starve to death. And I really could hang up, I'm sure your mind isn't on my lunch habits."

"I'd rather see you, but I know that's impossible." God, she couldn't know how badly he wanted to see her, talk to her in person.

There was a slight pause at the other end of the line. "There's something wrong, isn't there? I mean, *really* wrong."

"Maybe. I don't know. Okay, yes. Yes, if I can believe her, this is going to be a bad one. She really came out of left field on me with this one."

"Can you get a sitter for tonight? I mean, you don't have to tell me anything if you don't want to. I certainly understand. And we barely know each other—"

"I can be at your place by seven," he said before she could talk either one of them out of the idea. "I'll bring dinner. Do you like Mexican?"

"I like food, Nick. Whatever you want to eat is fine with me. I have to get back to work. I'll see you later?"

"Around seven, yes. And Claire? Thank you."

He cut the connection and dropped back onto the chaise, looking up through the canopy of old trees, not really seeing them, or the blue sky above them.

He had full custody of Sean. Sandy had signed away all of her rights to her son six long years ago. She never saw him, rarely remembered his birthday or Christmas. Hell, he kept a stash of extra presents in his bedroom closet, and if a present didn't show up from Sandy, he gave one of them to Sean, telling him it was from his mother. Not because he didn't want Sandy to look bad. Because he didn't want to see that sad look in his son's eyes.

No. Sandy didn't have a legal leg to stand on; she'd never get custody.

But she could conceivably get visitation rights. The young mother, depressed, confused, trapped in a loveless marriage, desperate for the generous financial settlement, not realizing what she was signing. All of that. It wasn't impossible.

Then what? She'd stick around just long enough to confuse Sean, screw with the kid's head and heart, and then take off again?

And then there was Claire. She'd come into his life at the worst possible moment. Except he couldn't think of Claire and not be glad she was in his life. What would Sandy's return do to them, to their chances for more than they already had together? The future he'd already foolishly begun to contemplate?

Nick sat up, stared into the middle distance. "What am I going to do?" he asked the air. "What in *hell* am I going to do?"

Claire looked at the table in her small dining area, and decided the flowers she'd picked up on the way home looked a little too...contrived. And they'd have to talk over the top of the arrangement, which was stupid.

She moved them to the bar that separated the dining space from the kitchen. Now the table looked fine. Simple dishes, simple glasses, a bottle of uncomplicated wine for those glasses cooling in the fridge. Or should it be open and breathing on the counter?

Maybe she needed to drink wine more often. Then she'd know.

"Stop it," she scolded herself, flicking a fork into line with its knife partner.

Leaving the table, she checked her reflection in the mirror hung above the long end of her L-shaped couches, to see that she didn't look any different than she had ten minutes earlier.

She'd unpinned her hair from the French twist, intending to leave it down, but then reconsidered. In the end, she settled on a compromise: she'd pulled her hair back from her face, and then clipped it in place, leaving most of it to fall free. She was wearing a simple A-line green linen skirt, a patterned shell and flat sandals. The working woman at home, at her leisure.

At least she hoped Nick would think she was relaxed.

Claire had spent the last twenty-four and more hours reliving her time with Nick. Sometimes she smiled. Sometimes she felt wistful. And more often than not, she felt heat running into her cheeks as she thought back on her behavior. Their behavior.

But she regretted not a single moment of their time together.

As Nick had said, they were adults. Adults made choices.

Hearts, however, worked independently of the choices of the mind, and never really planned ahead, thought about consequences.

Or the very real chance of being hurt.

He'd said his ex was out of his life, and had been since Sean was little more than a baby. And yet, within days of meeting him, being with him, his ex appeared to be back in the picture. Had he lied to her?

Men with sex on their minds often lied.

Not that she was an expert, but she had girlfriends. She'd heard the stories, wondered how so many otherwise intelligent women could be so gullible.

Like Janene, and the guy she had dated in secret for two years, believing that, although the guy still lived with his wife, they didn't share a bedroom, the marriage was all but over and he was just waiting until his daughter started high school before leaving for good. A good story—until Janene found out his wife was pregnant.

Or her friend from college, Edie, who'd confided to her just last year that the sex had never been better in her marriage than in the months before Aidan had admitted he'd been having an affair during all of those months, and was now leaving her for the other woman. Like he'd been comparison shopping, or something. Talk about your pond scum...

But Nick wasn't like that. He simply wasn't.

She'd heard his voice when he told her his ex had phoned him, the stunned disbelief in it.

The question was, did she really want to get involved in Nick's life? Her own life was running smoothly now, with no dramas, no problems. She'd worked hard for the peace she'd found. It was safe here, on the ground.

The sound of the doorbell shook her from her thoughts, her pulse immediately going into overdrive. So she counted to ten, quitting at six, and opened the door.

"Delivery boy," Nick said, holding up a large white plastic bag that was emitting decidedly enticing aromas. "I hope you like fajitas."

"Chicken or steak?" she asked him, standing back so he could come in while doing her best not to notice how absolutely gorgeous he was, or how much she wanted to, yes, jump his bones.

"I'm allowed in either way?" he asked her.

"It's seven o'clock and I haven't eaten since I managed half a bologna sandwich around noon. If you want to leave, you can. But the bag stays here."

"Then it's chicken. Oh, and hi, thanks for taking me in tonight." He leaned in, kissed her on the mouth, withdrawing before she was ready, so that she was left standing there with her eyes closed, her mouth still craving more.

By the time she'd recovered, Nick was unloading the bag, pulling out Styrofoam containers and arranging them on the table. She hastened over to help him.

"Wine's in the fridge. I hope I bought the right kind."

"Screw top or cork?" he asked her, straightening and pushing a hand through the hair that had fallen forward on his forehead.

"Cork," she said, guessing.

"Then you bought the right kind. That's as picky as I get about wine. I'll get it, you sit down."

The meal was pleasant. They talked about work, Sean's Healthy Living project for school and the best way to keep poster board from folding in half when set up in a tripod display on a cafeteria table, the President's upcoming visit to Allentown to kick off some small-business incentive just passed by the Congress and how traffic would be snarled all day.

They could talk about anything, move seamlessly from subject to subject. It was as if they'd known each other all of their lives. The meal disappeared, the level in the wine bottle went down, almost without them noticing.

By the time Claire picked up their plates and carried them into the kitchen, Nick was looking a lot more relaxed than he had when she'd opened the door to him. The tight lines around his mouth were gone, and the slight shadow had left his eyes.

Claire felt rather proud of herself about that.

Nick put the wine glasses down on the counter as she rinsed the plates and fitted them into the dishwasher. "Thanks, Claire, I know I needed that. I think I'm finally past the panic, and can maybe talk to you about Sandy's phone call without breaking things."

She rinsed and loaded the utensils and wine glasses before drying her hands on a dishtowel. "Since they'd be my things, I'm glad I could help. But you don't have to tell me if you don't want to. Maybe it would be better if you just tried to forget whatever it is until you feel better equipped to… to—"

"Not want to choke her with her own guitar strap?" he suggested as they returned to the living room.

"Okay, that would be a good reason," Claire said, smiling at him as she sat down on the couch, kicking off her sandals and pulling her legs up under her as she patted the cushion next to her, inviting him to join her. "It might also be a reason to tell me. You know, blow off some steam?"

"Yes. I'd like to do that."

She sat quietly and let him talk. She rubbed his back when he leaned forward, his elbows on his knees, his very real and logical concerns for Sean touching her heart.

He finished with Sandy's parting threat, that of hiring a lawyer.

"Do you really think she'll do that?"

"I don't know," Nick said, leaning back against the cushions, looking exhausted. "I've thought about wiring her some money, thinking that maybe that's what she's really after, and she's just using Sean as a club of sorts. But she could just as easily hire a lawyer with it."

"And a lawyer could take her money, and then turn around and accuse you of trying to buy her off," Claire pointed out carefully. "My vote would be no money. That is, not that I have a vote."

He took her hand, brought it to his lips. "I like that you're concerned. I really appreciate it."

She felt her cheeks coloring. "I appreciate that you thought to…to share with me."

"And thus ends the first annual convention of the Barrington-Ayers Mutual Appreciation Club." He pulled her close, whispering his next words into her ear. "But before we adjourn…"

She smiled as he tipped her chin up so that he could kiss her blissfully closed eyes, the tip of her nose, teasing her with small kisses before at last claiming her mouth.

All the passion she'd felt before came rushing back, but now that passion had taken on a deeper meaning, a rich fullness that could only come from more than mere sexual compatibility, which they had in abundance.

She stroked his cheek, but more to feel his closeness than to further their passion. She wanted to be here with him, yes, but she also wanted to be here *for* him. As she instinctively knew he would be there for her if she needed him.

This was all new to her. This more mature passion. This totally unselfish giving.

She felt tears welling up in her eyes, and welcomed them, even as she welcomed Nick's touch.

Over the weekend, they'd had sex.

Tonight, between them, they made love…

## Chapter Seven

"So?"

Claire finished retouching her lipstick in the mirror above the sinks in the community center lavatory, trying not to laugh at the anxious look on Marylou Smith-Bitters' face. Except for her forehead, of course, that couldn't wrinkle if she were offered a million dollars to wiggle her well-plucked eyebrows.

She closed the lipstick and returned it to her purse before answering. "You know, Marylou, my grandmother always had an answer for that question. So what? Sew buttons. I don't know what she meant, but I soon learned not to ask her questions that particular way."

Marylou grinned. "You're stalling. Good. That means it went well. Do I get details?"

Claire zipped shut her purse and turned around, leaning back against the countertop. "Uh-uh."

"Ah, even better. I get to make them up on my own. And I have a *very* good imagination."

"Good try, but you won't embarrass me into telling you anything, either." Claire headed for the door, as class would begin soon, but then turned around to face Marylou. "Thank you," she said simply. "For butting in."

"Me? Claire, sweetie, I don't butt in. I…all right. I butt in. You will admit, though, that I do it very well. I like to see people happy, that's all. And *how* they can be made happy is always so obvious to me." She shrugged her Armani-clad shoulders. "It's a gift."

Claire laughed. "It's something, that's for sure. I understand I have a new class member tonight. Also a gift from you."

"Evelina," Marylou said, following Claire out of the restroom. "She only gave birth a month ago, to just the most beautiful little boy. He looks like an angel from one of Michelangelo's paintings. Big brown eyes the size of saucers. You still have a minute—come see him."

"Come see him? He's here?"

"Don't panic, I know you can't have a baby in the classroom, or everyone would want to bring their own children, and then what could you get done, right? But Salvatore—Evelina's husband—takes

Nick's class, so it was either bring Stefano or Evelina couldn't take the class. So I…improvised."

They'd gotten to the registration desk by then, and Claire saw a good-looking young woman with a flattering mop of copper curls holding a blanket-wrapped bundle up against her shoulder, a mixture of soft affection and blind panic in her eyes.

"Chessie, support his head, for pity's sake," Marylou scolded the woman. "He's little, but babies are strong, and he could decide to perform a back flip."

The woman quickly put a hand to the back of the baby's head. "I told you I love babies, Marylou. Do you remember me saying anything about knowing how to take care of them? Because I sure don't."

"You're a woman, Chessie. It comes naturally."

"That's an old wives' tale, unfortunately, which is why I give my class," Claire said, immediately thinking of Nick's ex-wife, Sandy. "Hi, I'm Claire Ayers," she told Chessie. "May I see him?"

"Chessie Burton. Nice to meet you, Claire. And you can have him," Chessie said, gratefully handing over the infant. "They're so…breakable."

Claire cradled the baby in her arms and smiled down at him. He did look like one of Michelangelo's cherubs. Her eyes ran over him professionally. His color was good, he held his little hands in tight fists, and he seemed to be trying to follow voices with his eyes. Just a nice, healthy, precious little bundle of love.

"I brought Chessie along to help me watch Stefano while Evelina and Salvatore are in class,"

Marylou said. "I didn't realize she was incompetent, did I, Chessie?"

"Har-har," Chessie grumbled, folding her hands under her breasts. "The things you rope me into during a weak moment, Marylou..."

"Just ignore her, Claire. She's really a sweetheart. Chessie owns Second Chance Bridal, you know. It's just the most marvelous shop, and dedicated to second-time-around brides, who often aren't comfortable in regular bridal salons. Isn't that just a genius idea? I've been her customer. Twice."

"One more time, and I may begin offering her a discount," Chessie said, her cornflower blue eyes dancing.

"An interesting offer, but I finally got it right with Ted. Sometimes the first one just doesn't stick, does it? Like, oh, like for Nick," Marylou said, and now *her* eyes were dancing.

"And we're off," Chessie said, as if she'd witnessed Marylou in action before, and rather enjoyed the experience. "This would be Nick Barrington, right, Marylou? Barb's cousin, who came with her to the salon? The one you said you had just the perfect woman for? *That* Nick Barrington?"

"Maybe," Marylou said, taking Stefano from Claire. "You'll be late for class, honey," she added, expertly snuggling the now sleeping baby. Or perhaps using him as a shield.

Claire and Chessie exchanged glances, and a friendship was born.

"It was nice meeting you, Claire," Chessie said. "Maybe we can all get together someday for lunch. My salon closes from twelve-thirty to two every day."

"I'm afraid I rarely get to leave the office for lunch," Claire said, genuinely disappointed. "But perhaps we three could have dinner one night?"

"Wonderful! Tomorrow night," Marylou said quickly. Deftly balancing Stefano on her shoulder, she reached into her purse and pulled out an ivory-colored business card with gold edging, and handed it to Claire. "We'll meet at the salon, all right? It's central to your office and my hairdresser, and you really should see it, Claire. It's just a lovely place. I'm having my roots touched up tomorrow at three, so we could all meet at, say, five-thirty? I'll make reservations. Oh, I know! Do you like Italian? There's this lovely restaurant in Bethlehem called Stefano's I like a lot. Isn't that perfect? Almost like a *sign*."

Chessie stifled a giggle with her fist as she turned her reaction into a cough.

"Uh…okay. Sure," Claire said, nodding her suddenly whirling head. "Tomorrow. Well, I've got to run."

She was still within earshot when she heard Chessie say, "And now I owe you five bucks. You were right, Marylou, as usual. It's perfect for her."

*It's perfect for her?* What was perfect for her?

Claire shrugged her shoulders and kept walking,

mentally shifting gears to her topic for tonight's class: ear infections. She lived such a glamorous life...

He watched her walk toward him, threading her way through the students just recently released from their classrooms.

She amazed him.

There was this...calmness about her. She stood out in any crowd. There was some sort of *aura* she projected, one that had nothing to do with how beautiful she was, or the clothes she wore. No. It was more than that.

Claire was the sort of person others automatically looked to for answers, for direction. For reassurance. If selected to serve on a jury, she would be unanimously nominated to be the foreperson. If a plane went down in the Hudson, you could count on her to not panic, to be the one others looked to for rescue. If the carefully constructed world you'd built for your son was in danger of coming apart, Claire could be counted on to remain objective, be supportive.

People couldn't learn to be like Claire Ayers. You were either born with this special gift, or you weren't. And like most people like her, she had no idea how very special she was.

He'd needed her last night. Her calmness, her competence. He'd been in a near panic ever since Sandy's phone call, whether that was a rational reaction or not. He hadn't cared about himself—he had survived Sandy, and he was a big boy, he could handle his own problems.

But not Sean.

Nick's son was his world, and now that world might be threatened. Rational thought hadn't been at the top of Nick's list of things to do after Sandy's phone call.

A week ago, his reaction would have been to call his lawyer, demand a miracle, no matter what the cost.

Yesterday, his only thought had been to talk to Claire Ayers. That hadn't been fair of him, he knew that, but it had felt so natural to go to her, to talk with her, to sort out his feelings and, yes, to have her rub his back, touch his hand, the physical contact, that so-human contact, making him feel less alone.

He hadn't gone to her with the idea that they'd have sex again. Sex had been the last thing on his mind, for crying out loud. But when comforting had somehow segued to something more intimate the shift had been seamless, a natural progression.

Their pace had been more relaxed and unhurried than before, each touch more deliberate, to be slowly savored. He'd taken his time with her, rousing her even as she calmed him, until their bodies found their combined rhythms.

He'd worshiped her body with his mouth, his hands. Kissing her everywhere, touching her everywhere. She hadn't been passive, but she seemed to know that he needed to be the aggressor, needed to be in control of something in his life at that moment.

She gave to him, opened herself to him, took him deep inside her. Holding him, unselfishly lending him her strength. Making him—God help him or damn him for a fool—remember he was a man, that he had strengths of his own.

Somehow she'd sensed when he'd moved beyond needing and progressed to wanting. Madly, deeply, wanting. Wanting her. *Only her.* Only then did she become the aggressor, openly sexual. Driving him wild, taking them both out of the world that was and into a new, boundless universe of sensual pleasure.

And when at last they came back to Earth, replete, holding each other, whispering nonsense things to each other, smiling, even laughing, Nick knew himself to be stronger than he'd been, more centered and less worried, better prepared to face his problem with Sandy head-on, and protect his son.

Because now, whether or not either of them had said so in more than physical ways, Nick had realized he was no longer facing that problem alone.

He pressed a thumb and forefinger to the bridge of his nose, reluctantly pushing away thoughts of last night, and smiled at Claire as he held up a white paper bag so she could see it.

"*Mille-feuille, mon chère?*" he said as she looked at the bag, and then inhaled deeply.

"If that means do I want to know what that heavenly smell is, yes, I do," she told him, reaching for the bag. "I missed lunch again today, thanks to

Jaime Adams and his desire to see how many peas he could fit in his ear. Gimme!"

"You don't even want to compliment me on my French?"

She reached again for the bag, this time managing to grab it. "Not particularly, no. Oh, Napoleons. Why didn't you just say so? I *love* Napoleons. Let's go to the cafeteria and snag some forks."

"You didn't eat lunch, and you want a Napoleon for dinner? I think you're overlooking several other food groups, Ms. Ayers." He grabbed the bag once more.

She tipped her head as she glared at him. "I'm a grown-up, Nick. One of the benefits of being a grown-up is getting to break a rule now and then. But you're right."

"I've also got an ulterior motive," he told her as they turned in unison and headed for the cafeteria. "I want to tell you about Sandy's follow-up call this afternoon, if you don't mind."

She shot him a concerned look. "Nope. I can't tell by looking at you if this is going to be good news or bad news."

They picked up trays and got in line behind the leotard-clad exercise ladies, Claire hanging back a little so that he had to get into line first. He hid a smile. "It's half of one, half of the other. She's flying in to Allentown from Vegas on Friday."

Claire only nodded, as if she'd been expecting this possibility. "And the good news?"

"She promises not to come to see Sean or try to contact him in any way until I've talked to her and I agree that she can. And then we move on to the dilemna, I suppose. Do I tell Sean? What do I tell Sean?"

They both turned to look at his son, sitting at his usual table with his friends from the karate class. It was chocolate ice cream again tonight. Nick didn't know if "real men" presoaked, but he'd learned how to do it.

"Thanks, Ruth," Claire said, grabbing the plate holding two slices of plain pizza and quickly lowering it to Nick's tray. "Pretend it's yours," she said quietly. "And then order, I don't know, yogurt or something for me."

Nick looked at her, glanced to his left to the petite blond whose heavily made-up face wasn't made prettier by her sneering smile, or her condescending *tsk-tsk*, and then looked at Claire again. "You're kidding, right?" he asked her in a whisper. "You care what that semi-anorexic woman thinks?"

"Well, I am going to eat at least half of one of those Napoleons, you know, so I shouldn't really have too many other carbs," she said, and then shook her head in disgust. "What, am I nuts? Ruth? Ruth! How about two more slices for Mr. Barrington now that I have mine. With pepperoni, please."

Nick had laid the pastry bag he'd gotten courtesy of Salvatore on his own tray, but now Claire picked it up, unrolled the top, and stepped past him, to all but stick the open bag beneath the blonde's nose. "Here. Inhale. Sinful, isn't it? That's my dessert, and I'm going to eat it all. What's yours? Or do you guys just go out on the lawn after this and graze?"

Nick tried to cover his bark of laughter by turning it into a cough. But it didn't work and he gave it up. Instead, he leaned against the railing that served as a sort of cattle-shoot for the cafeteria line and laughed until tears came to his eyes.

The blond woman picked up her tray and nearly ran after her friends, probably in a hurry to get away from the lunatics, and Claire covered her face with her hands. "Oh, why did I *do* that? I must be really, *really* hungry."

"Remind me to always keep you well fed," Nick told her as he paid for their meals and they headed for what some romantic sort might have begun to call *their table*. Sean was already sitting there. "Hi, Sean. You boys are all done?"

"No, just me. You've got one of those bags from Mr. Georgio's bakery again. What's in it? Donuts? Hi, Ms. Ayers."

"Not this time, champ," Nick said, passing over the bag.

"Oh, wow, *mille-feuille.*" He grinned at his father. "*J'irai nous obtiens quelques fourchettes.*"

"*Très bon, et arrêt montrant au loin devant la dame,*" Nick responded, rubbing his son's head before watching him head for the counter and the containers of plastic utensils.

"He knows French? And you taught him, I'm sure. I'm so impressed. What did you two say to each other?"

Nick picked up his first slice of pizza. "Well, it probably sounds better in French, but he said he'd go get us some forks, and I told him to stop showing off in front of the lady. I've spoken French to him ever since he was born, because that's how my mother did it with my sister and me."

"I'm so jealous. The only other language I know, and only thanks to memorization, is Latin. You know, *musculus latissimus dorsi, rigor mortis, placebo.* Not a lot of call for any of that at parties."

"The *rigor mortis* especially, I'd imagine," Nick teased as Sean came back to the table with three forks, a plastic knife and some paper plates. "Thanks, Champ."

"I've got my test Thursday after class, Dad. Me and Jacob."

"Jacob and I," Nick corrected automatically. "You think you're ready?"

Sean spoke around a mouthful of creamy pastry. "Sensei says I am." He turned to Claire. "Will you come and watch me, Ms. Ayers? I'm really good."

Nick and Claire exchanged glances, and he nodded.

"Why, thank you, Sean. I'd love to. Will you be breaking boards on Thursday night?"

Sean launched into a description of what he and Jacob would and would not be doing in order to qualify for the next level of training, answering

Claire's questions as their dessert disappeared, the subject having changed to that of the movie father and son were going to see that weekend, and would Ms. Ayers want to maybe come with them?

Nick just sat back and listened. It was as if he wasn't even there. He hadn't realized how starved his son must be for the attention of a female, a softer presence in his life.

Then, unbidden, he thought about his ex-wife. How would Sean feel about seeing Sandy, having Sandy possibly back in his life?

And why was he less apprehensive about introducing Claire into Sean's life than he was about allowing him to see his birth mother?

"Claire, there you are. I need you to come with me for a moment, please."

"Something wrong, Marylou?" Nick asked, looking up at her as she approached the table.

She leaned down, speaking softly. "Claire, I think there's something wrong with Stefano. But I want you to look at him before I say anything to Salvatore or Evelina."

Claire immediately put her hand down, grabbed her purse and briefcase, but then hesitated. "Uh-uh, Marylou. One of them has to ask me to look at Stefano. That's the only way. What's the problem? I only saw him for a few moments, but he certainly looked healthy to me."

Marylou looked across the table at Sean. "*Pas en face de l'enfant.*"

Nick pulled his wallet from his pocket and extracted a few bills. "Here you go, Sean. Let me treat you and the boys to hot pretzels, or something. Stay here with them. We'll be right back."

But Sean dug in his heels. "Not in front of the child. That's me. What can't she say in front of me? You always said that was rude, Dad. Speaking another language in company if everyone else didn't speak the same language."

Marylou's eyes widened. "He speaks French? Somebody could have warned me, you know. But you're right, Sean. I was being rude, and I apologize most sincerely. Now, take the money your father is holding, and then take a hike back to your buddies."

Nick laughed, shaking his head. "You're one of a kind, Marylou, I'll give you that," he said as Sean ran off to his buddies. "Let's go."

"Chessie's got him in your classroom, Claire, stalling for us with Salvatore and Evelina, so that they don't take him home," Marylou told them as they made their way down the corridor. "She's pretty good at stalling, but it could come down to a tug-of-war if we don't rescue her."

"Marylou, do you want to tell me what you think is wrong with Stefano?" Claire asked her as they picked up their pace.

The older woman stopped, looked at Nick. "It's pretty personal," she warned him. "Maybe you want to wait here."

"He's a baby. What the hell could be pretty

personal about a—oh," Nick said, frowning. "You want to get a little more specific?"

Marylou shrugged. "He doesn't look right, Claire," she said, wringing her hands. "I mean, I was changing his diaper—Chessie drew a line in the sand on that one—and when I pulled down his little diaper? Now, I may not have the equipment myself, but I've seen my share—stop laughing, Nick!" She turned pleading eyes to Claire. "Can't you just take a look?"

"If the parents agree," Claire said again.

They entered the classroom to see Chessie holding on to Stefano, rather like Grim Death, Nick thought, and Evelina gesturing that she wanted her baby.

"Oh, thank God," Chessie said when she spied them. "I feel like a kidnapper. Here, take him. The things you get me into, Marylou."

Stefano was all but shoved into Claire's arms, and she smiled rather weakly before appealing to Nick to explain to the parents that Marylou had wanted her to examine the child.

It took some time, and some tears from the worried mother, but at last Claire was allowed to lay Stefano on the changing table that was part of the equipment in her classroom. Evelina unwrapped the baby while Claire pulled on exam gloves she'd taken from her briefcase, asking Salvatore to instruct Evelina to take down the baby's diaper.

Nick stood behind Clare as everyone else crowded around the changing table, all of them hovering close, rather like passersby rubbernecking to see a fender bender on the thruway.

"You see it, Claire?" Marylou asked anxiously. "I see it."

"So do I. Good catch, Marylou," Claire said, taping the diaper back into place without physically examining the child. "Salvatore? Evelina? Your baby is fine," she said in a competent and yet soothing voice. "What you're seeing? It's called a hydrocele. A sort of fluid-filled sac located along the spermatic cord and visible in the scrotum. It's fairly common in infants, and we only do something about it if we think it's going to cause a problem. Then it's a simple repair, usually performed at an in-and-out surgical center."

Salvatore nodded furiously, and then quickly translated for Evelina. The young woman's bottom lip quivered, but then she picked up her son and thanked Claire. "You will do this for our Stefano?"

"No, I'm not a surgeon, Evelina. I'd like you to bring Stefano to our offices tomorrow so that my brother, who is a pediatrician, can examine him, check his general health and then recommend a surgeon if he feels a repair necessary. Which, remember, it might not be."

"We must take Stefano to the clinic," Salvatore told her sadly. "We don't have the money for you or your brother."

"Yes they do," Marylou stated firmly. "Just start a tab for me, Claire, all right?" She pressed a kiss on the top of the sleeping Stefano's head. "Auntie Marylou is going to take care of everything."

Chessie sidled up next to Nick and Claire. "She means it, too. Glenda the Good Witch, in designer clothes."

Nick and Claire returned to the cafeteria to collect Sean, who had a million questions for her, all of which she answered very matter-of-factly.

"Okay," Sean said, nodding solemnly, as if he approved. "Thanks." Then he ran ahead with his friend Jacob, saying he'd meet his dad at the car.

"He took that well," Nick remarked in some surprise.

"You don't mind that I was so frank with him? I've found it better not to fib to children. For one thing, they can always tell."

"No, I think he appreciated it. And you were great with Stefano's parents. You've got a terrific bedside manner, Ms. Ayers. I enjoyed watching you."

"Why, thank you, Mr. Barrington," she said, reaching into her purse for her keys. "If we ever have Take Your Boyfriend To Work Day, I'll be sure to invite you."

Nick looked across the now nearly empty parking lot to see that Sean was already in the car, his back to him. He maneuvered Claire so that her back was against her car door and moved close, brought his face to within inches of hers in the near-dark.

"Does that also make you my girlfriend?" he

asked, half-teasingly. "Will you wear my class ring around your neck on a chain?"

"And write your name on all my notebooks, sure," she answered, stroking his cheek. "You'd better go. Sean's waiting for you."

Nick's full attention was now trained on her smiling mouth. "He can wait another minute…"

Nick opened his own car door five minutes later, and slid onto the front seat. "Sorry, Champ. Ms. Ayers and I were talking."

"How do you do that, Dad, when you're kissing each other?"

Nick's hand stilled in the act of inserting the key into the ignition, and he turned to look at his son. He remembered Claire's statement that it was better not to fib to children—mostly because they usually knew when someone was lying to them.

"And how do you feel about that, Sean?" he asked his son.

Sean shrugged.

"Come on," Nick urged, "you can talk to me about anything. You know that, don't you?"

"Yeah," Sean said at last, so quietly Nick had to lean closer to hear him. "I think…I think it would be neat to have a mom. I mean, Mom doesn't count, because she's not here, so I think it would be good if we found someone else, who would be here. You know?"

Sean was looking at him now, his eyes so young, so vulnerable.

"Yeah, Champ. I know. Let's just…see how this works out, okay? But I have your approval?"

Sean turned back to the handheld video game in his lap. "Sure. But thanks for asking."

Nick smiled all the way home.

## Chapter Eight

Claire pulled up in front of Second Chance Bridal and stepped out of her car, smiling at the sight of the huge Victorian house Chessie Burton had converted into her place of business.

The building had Old World charm in massive doses, along with a hint of whimsy in the soft violet painted clapboard and dark green trim on the fretwork. As she walked up the path to the door, she could see that there were gowns displayed in the first-floor windows that were framed by delicate white lace curtains.

It was all so sweet, and charming, and welcoming.

Places like this were dangerous. They made you believe in the fantasy.

Claire climbed the broad wooden steps and noticed the Closed sign on the door, but before she could wonder if she should knock, the door opened and Chessie poked her head outside.

"Hi, you're right on time. I was just coming to take the sign off the door, realizing you might wonder if I'd forgotten. But I didn't. Come on, come in."

"I don't know, Chessie. Last time I was in one of these places I was on my way to making a big mistake."

"You, too?" Chessie called back over her shoulder as she walked away from the open door, obviously confident Claire was going to follow her. "The very first gown in my inventory was the one I was going to wear for my wedding. Of course, that was before Rick ditched me for my maid of honor the night before the wedding. Sounds like a soap opera, doesn't it?"

"You don't sound too heartbroken," Claire pointed out as she looked around the large room, admiring the contents of the glass-topped cases, the cozy arrangement of chairs around a large fireplace, the tall vase of fresh flowers on the table between them. "Oh, this is lovely."

"Thank you, and no, I'm not. I was, and I thought my life was over at the time, but now I know I was lucky. Imagine if we'd gone through with the wedding? I mean, then I would have had to kill him, wouldn't I?"

Chessie turned her full one-hundred-watt smile on Claire. "Kidding. Just kidding. And it was all a long time ago. Over five years. And look at me now—I've got my own business."

"Did you ever sell your gown?"

"I did. I don't believe in bad-luck dresses or anything like that. I simply said yes to the wrong man. It wasn't the gown's fault. Marylou's in the back, checking out some new stock that came in today. She seems to think I need her seal of approval. Soda?"

"Uh, no, thank you." Claire looked at the gowns in the window. One was a waltz-length peach-blush creation with a lace overlay, and the other a more traditional gown, with a trumpet skirt. "So this is what the well-dressed second-chance bride is wearing these days?"

"Sometimes. It's different for every bride. Do you want to see Barb's? Nick's cousin. Marylou said you're going to the wedding with him."

"How would she know that I'm—never mind. I probably don't want to know. But, yes, I would like to see it, as long as we've got time?"

"Plenty. Follow me," Chessie said, heading toward a door at the back of the room. "Would I be nosy if I asked about your marriage? I'm getting the idea it wasn't a lot of laughs?"

"You could say that. Along with having the shelf life of a cantaloupe. We simply weren't on the same page as to how our marriage should work. He's getting married again, and I wish both of them all the luck in the world." How freeing it was to say those words, and really mean them. And then she stopped dead, and simply stared. "Oh, isn't that *gorgeous.*"

Claire touched the skirt of the gown that was hanging prominently in a room lined with racks of gowns, all the others safely zipped up inside clear plastic garment bags.

Not that Claire noticed. She just couldn't look away from this one gown. This one perfect gown.

"Don't you just love it?" Chessie said, smiling brightly. "It's a showstopper. I love a dropped waist, and how do you say no to a ball-gown skirt like that, the chapel train? It's silk over satin, and the draping is— that seed pearl clip on the left hip, the folds all falling from it? Elegant is the only word I can find. There's no bling with this gown, just quiet, understated elegance. Classy and classic, and slightly European."

Claire touched the strapless bodice, all of it covered in a swirling vine-like design of fine embroidery and seed pearls that matched the color of the gown. "What color is this?"

"In the olden days, I think it was considered to be tea-stained. I've dipped more than one veil in tea to get this color, myself. Not really beige, darker than ivory, almost ecru, but not exactly that, either. Now we call it champagne. Perfect for a second wedding, don't you think?"

"I don't know about that. I just think it's perfect, period. What a fun job you have, Chessie. It must be like playing dress-up every day when you come to work."

Chessie's expression went all soft, and Claire liked her even more. "I do get a huge kick out of making people happy. And when a bride puts on the right gown—when I've picked the right gown for her—you can just *tell*. I mean, I may not be curing some terrible disease or making the world safe for democracy or anything like that, but I'll take it. Oh, Marylou, there you are. The new stock is out here. What were you doing in the back room?"

Marylou closed the door to the back room and smiled brightly at the two of them. "Just looking at Barb's gown, now that it's all pressed and ready to go. Do you want to see it, Claire?"

Claire shook her head. "Now that I think about it, I believe I'd rather first see Nick's cousin in it when she comes down the aisle. Looking at it now seems sort of…intrusive."

"Good point. Okay," Chessie said, rubbing her hands together. "Is everybody ready to go? Oh, and how could I forget? Does little Stefano need surgery? Please say he doesn't."

"It's too soon for a definitive answer," Claire told both women, "but, so far, no. We'll keep watching him. Marylou, that was really nice of you, to offer to pay for Stefano's visits. You're something else."

"Yes, I get that a lot. But it isn't always a compliment." Marylou picked up her purse, but then stopped to fluff out the skirt of the ball gown. "You know, I've been *dying* to see this one on somebody."

"Me, too," Chessie agreed. "I haven't put it on anyone yet, and that's unusual, since I've had it here for over a month. I haven't even tried it on myself. But not just anyone can wear something so dramatic. It has to be the right person, or the bride would disappear and nobody would see anything but the gown."

"You're right. I would have tried it on, but I'm not tall enough to carry it off. It takes a special person to wear this one. Tall, definitely, but also quietly elegant. I'm a little too flamboyant for a stunner like this. Not to mention bony." Then she turned and smiled at Claire. "You know what? I'll bet you could do it. You're exactly the right type for a gown like this. Come on, let's do it. You'll have a ball. It's such fun to play dress-up."

Claire laughed and rolled her eyes. No wonder the gown had been hanging in plain sight when she'd entered the back room. Marylou had put it there on purpose. "Marylou, I've seen two-year-olds with more guile. No, I am not going to try on that gown for you. Seriously, I'm not."

Marylou shrugged and smiled. "Too obvious, huh?"

"As a big red clown nose in the middle of your face," Chessie said, laughing. "I had a feeling it wouldn't work. But I'll hand it to you, buddy, you're always thinking."

"Oh, all right. Party poopers, that's what you two

are, you know. But never let it be said I don't know when I'm licked. Come on, let's all go together in my car. That way we won't lose each other in traffic."

Several hours of friendly conversation often punctuated by laughter later, and with three glasses of wine and a plate of spaghetti bolognaise under her belt, Claire was standing in a dressing room at Second Chance Bridal, looking at herself in the gown, wondering if she really looked as good as she thought she might, or if the wine was playing tricks on her.

This was all Marylou's fault. Or, Claire admitted to herself, all Marylou's devious plan. The gown hanging in plain sight. The seed, well planted. The off-hand suggestion that they all go to the restaurant in her car. The two expensive bottles of wine she'd ordered—one red, one white—and then pushed on Chessie and Claire, saying she'd forgotten she'd taken a decongestant, and couldn't drink any of it herself. "Can't let it go to waste, now can we?"

Oh, the woman was a menace. Brilliant, but a menace. And maybe Claire had been more willing than she'd wanted to admit.

"Okay, that was fun," Claire said, annoyed that her voice seemed a little shaky. "Now get me out of this thing and let's find some coffee somewhere."

"I've already got a pot brewing upstairs," Chessie told her. Claire had already learned that Chessie lived above the shop. "But first, since you're already in the gown, let me see if I can recreate the look a bit from the catalog. Can you take down your hair? Yeah, like that. Now fluff it out, still keeping it away from your forehead and—yes, that's it. Perfect. Now for the earrings. These aren't exactly the same as in the photograph, but they're close enough."

Claire eyed the large earrings with some trepidation. They were at least two inches long, diamond-shaped, all constructed out of a sort of dull gold filigree in an open basket-weave design, and touched with tiny rhinestones. She expected them to be very heavy, but she barely felt them as Chessie clipped them to her ears.

"Yes, exactly the right touch of bling. I'm going to put them away, not sell them to anyone but whoever buys the gown," Chessie said as she stepped back, nodding her head. "These guys definitely know what they're doing. No necklace, no gloves, no veil. And yet every inch a bride. Perfect for a second wedding— I'd say formal, no matter if it's small or large, and absolutely a candlelight ceremony. This is definitely going to take a special bride. Thanks so much for doing this for me, Claire. How do you feel in it? It's a lot of material, but the design should have the weight of the skirt cleverly distributed over the hips thanks to the dropped waist. You shouldn't feel the weight."

Claire pressed her lips together, slowly shook her head. Words simply wouldn't come to her. She didn't recognize this sophisticated-looking woman reflected in the mirror.

But she liked her. She liked her very, very much.

She'd liked her wedding gown, although she'd always felt she'd…settled. But she'd been so busy with her last classes, with finding an apartment, interviewing for positions. The gown had just been another chore to check off before moving on to the next thing. And there'd been that slowly growing unease about Steven, and his not always amusing jokes about how maybe she didn't want to find a better job, but would rather stay home and be a real wife.

If Claire felt any "weight" now, it was from the mistakes of the past. Mistakes she didn't plan to repeat. Because it wasn't the ring, it wasn't the gown, it wasn't the shower and the just-right wedding favors, or even the ceremony itself. It was the man. If you didn't get that right, nothing else mattered.

"I…I want to take this off now."

"Are you sure?" Marylou asked her, bending to fluff out the train. "If I looked that good in something, I'd never take it off. How about we see how it would bustle for the reception? That's always tricky, and it's good to know how to do it before trying it on the client, right, Chessie?"

"No, I mean it. I need to get out of this gown. Now."

Chessie hurried over to her, undoing the back of the gown and then instructing her to bend her knees so that she could lift the heavy creation up and over her head.

Crossing her arms over the ridiculously risqué bustier she wore, Claire bent forward and took several deep breaths, trying to get her emotions under control.

"You and your bright ideas, Marylou," Chessie

grumbled, leading Claire to a chair and all but pushing her into it.

"I'm so sorry, sweetheart," Marylou said, going down on her knees in front of the chair and taking Claire's hands in hers. "I just can't seem to help myself. But I shouldn't have done it. I know I was wrong."

Claire took another breath as she shook her head, unwanted tears stinging at the back of her eyes. "No, Marylou," she said, trying to keep her voice steady. Was it the wine? No. Not the wine. "You weren't wrong. I…I just don't know what I'm going to do. I love him. I know it's too soon, I know it's not logical. But I love him. If I'm crying, it has nothing to do with the gown. It's Nick."

"What about Nick?" Marylou asked, squeezing her hands. "Don't tell me he isn't crazy about you, because I may not always be right, but I know I'm not wrong this time. It's like each of you was just waiting for the other one to come into your lives. Fate. Kismet. All that good stuff. And he goes all gooey-eyed every time he looks at you."

Claire smiled wanly as she accepted the tissue Chessie held out to her, and wiped at her eyes. "Nick couldn't go gooey-eyed if he tried."

"You know what I mean. And you love him. I'm looking for the downside in all of this, sweetheart, and I'm not seeing it."

"His ex-wife is coming back to town on Friday," Claire said quietly, between tears. "To…to see Sean and be a mother to him again, or so she says. Nick and Sandy didn't just divorce. She left him—just took off. He might have unresolved issues with her he doesn't think he has. And then there's Sean. He and I have hit it off really well, but now his mother…it's just all so complicated. And definitely happening too fast."

"I agree that the timing could have been better," Chessie said as she motioned for Claire to stand up, so she could step out of the net half-slip.

"I know. And I don't cry. I *never* cry. This is all that wine you kept pushing on me, Marylou. I shouldn't have told you about Sandy. I didn't even realize how much it bothers me that she's coming back here, upsetting everyone. And it's really…it's really none of my business."

"Of course it's your business," Marylou protested, handing over more tissues she'd pulled from the box Chessie was holding. "If you love him, it's your business. Or are you thinking you'll just walk away now that the ex is showing up, never even telling Nick how you feel about him?"

"I…I think he knows. We…we get along really well."

"Really? And I know what that translates to. Good for you."

"Leave it to you, Marylou. You know what we all need? We need coffee," Chessie announced solemnly, turning Claire around so that she could unhook the corset. "Nice big pot of coffee. Lots of coffee, lots of talking. And then one of my nightshirts for each of you, and beds for all of us. Marylou, you agree?"

"Are you kidding? You couldn't get me out of here tonight at the point of a gun. I don't know who this Sandy is, or why she left Nick and her own son, but she's no match for the three of us. We'll figure something out. Now don't yell at me, Claire, and don't you laugh at me, Chessie, but I think we should probably start thinking about Claire just flat-out telling Nick the truth, telling him that she loves him. I mean, unless we can think of something better…"

"Are we going to see Ms. Ayers tonight, Dad? She's going to come to my testing, isn't she? She said she was going to. She wouldn't say that if she wasn't going to come, would she?"

Nick shot his son a quick sideways look as they made their way through traffic on their way to the community center.

"She said she was going to be there, Champ. This is important to you? That Ms. Ayers is there?"

Sean fussed with the red belt tied around his waist. He'd trade it in for a brown one if he passed his tests tonight. "Yeah, I guess so. Jacob's mom is coming, and his grandmom, too. And his grandpop. And his sister Julie, and his cousin Bobbie. Not his brother Christopher because, you know, he's only a baby, so Jacob's dad is staying home with him. But that's okay, because Jacob's mom is taking video."

"Uh-huh," Nick said thoughtfully. Tonight was

clearly Big Stuff for his son. He should have at least called Barb and Skip. Why hadn't he thought of that? Why hadn't he thought about the damn video camera? Every time he thought he was doing a good job as a single parent, bam, something like this came up to kick him in the teeth. "You know that your grandparents would be here if they could. And your Aunt Catherine."

"I know. They can't help it that they don't live here. It's okay."

No, it wasn't okay. Sean needed a cheering section. He deserved one. Maybe if he hadn't been so obsessed with worrying what trick Sandy was up to, he would have remembered that, for Sean, this was a big night, a huge step upward in his training.

"You and Ms. Ayers like each other, don't you?" Sean asked after another fairly uncomfortable silence.

"Yes," Nick answered warily, "we like each other. Why?"

"I don't know," Seam mumbled. "Do you love each other?"

Nick congratulated himself silently that he hadn't run off the road. "Are you asking this because you saw me kissing Ms. Ayers the other night?"

Sean shrugged. "I suppose. So, do you love her? Jacob said his mom and dad kiss all the time. It really grosses him out."

"Well, then, Ms. Ayers and I will try not to gross you out. As for loving Claire? It's kind of early days for that, Champ. We've only know each other a week. Some things take more time. Is that it? Are we clear on this now?"

"I guess so."

This time, Nick didn't congratulate himself. Because he was pretty sure Sean had at least one more zinger in his pocket, ready to launch at him.

And it didn't take long before his son took out that zinger and zapped him with it.

"So, Dad. How long does it take?"

"How long does it take for what?"

"To know if you're in love with somebody."

"That's a very good question, son. A very good question."

"But you don't know the answer?"

"I'm not sure," Nick answered, not entirely honestly. But how do you tell a child that sometimes it takes a look, a moment and no more, and you know? You just know.

"Okay," Sean said, nodding. "Just let me know when you do."

"I'll be sure to do that," Nick said as he pulled into the parking lot, grateful he'd soon be in class, where the questions were easier. He went on the lookout for Claire's car as he pulled into a parking spot, but it wasn't parked in its usual space. She was probably just running late.

Sean sat up very straight on the front seat and looked around the lot. "Ms. Ayers isn't here, Dad. And it's almost seven o'clock. She should be here by now, shouldn't she?"

"She'll be here, Champ," Nick said with all the confidence he could manage. "Remember, she teaches tonight. Come on, let's get inside."

He put his hand on Sean's shoulder and they entered the building together, along with others heading for the classrooms.

"Over here, Nick," Chessie Burton said, waving to them from the registration desk. "I've got a message for you."

"Chessie," Nick said, steering Sean toward the desk. "Don't tell me you're babysitting again tonight."

"No, no more of that. Evelina found a woman in their apartment building who's agreed to watch Stefano, thank goodness. This time I'm here taking Marylou's place—she's so lucky I have no life. Anyway, Claire had an emergency at the hospital or something, and Marylou's going to take over the child-care class for her until she can get here. Oh, that's the message. Claire says she'll be here, but she'll be late. She asked Marylou to pass the message on to you, because she had to go, but she needed to be sure her classroom was covered, so that's why she called Marylou, and not you. Yeah," Chessie ended, looking up toward the ceiling, as if checking some unseen notes up there, to be sure she'd delivered the entire message, "that's all of it."

"I'm going to go to class," Sean said quietly, and turned to leave.

"Hey, don't go all doom and gloom on me, Champ," Nick told him. "She'll be here."

"Right." Sean turned once more, and shuffled away, his shoulders slumping.

"What's wrong, Nick?"

He raked a hand through his hair, and then shook his head in disgust. "Me, that's what's wrong. Sean and Jacob have their qualification test tonight after karate class, and Claire promised she'd be there. And, thanks to me, if she's not, then I'll be the only one there to watch him. The other kid's whole family is showing up. Probably bringing balloons, or something. Making me look even worse."

"Ouch. That's not good. Poor kid, poor daddy. But I'm sure Claire hasn't forgotten. She'll be here if she can. And Marylou and I will certainly stick around, if that helps?"

"That would be great, yes. Thanks. Well, I'd better get going." He took a few steps before he turned back to Chessie. "I'm taking a wild shot here, but you wouldn't happen to have a video camera with you, would you?"

Chessie grinned. "Sure, don't you? Your cell phone, Nick. You can probably take video with it."

He gave himself a mental slap to the forehead. "Now why didn't I think of that?"

"Men never think of everything. That's why they need women. We're much better in a crisis," Chessie teased, and then turned away to help a young woman who had come up to the registration desk.

With one last look toward the doorway, hoping to see Claire walking into the building, Nick headed for his classroom, the crestfallen look on his son's face still very clear in his mind. There had to be something he could do.

Claire ran into the community center clutching the small bag holding the first three volumes of a series of adventure books one of the mothers at the office had told her were the rage right now with nine-to-eleven-year-old boys.

She was late, almost too late to do anything more for her class than hope that Marylou hadn't ditched the lesson plan on childhood nutrition she'd faxed over to her, and she'd step inside the classroom in time to see her friend leading a Conga line, or something.

It was sort of funny, in some odd way, Claire had thought on her way to the community center. She'd been delayed by emergencies when she and Steven were married, and had resented feeling that she then needed to rush home, full of apologies for doing her job.

But tonight? Taking the chance of disappointing Sean? She hadn't been able to drive fast enough, her thoughts all on the child and not at all on her already long day, her aching back or any notion of just giving the evening a skip and going home to a nice warm bath.

"How's it going?" she asked Chessie as she trotted into the building. "What's she doing?"

"You don't really want me to answer that, right?" Chessie said, getting to her feet, following along behind Claire. "Just keep going straight, to the cafeteria. She took your class there."

Claire slowed down, suddenly reluctant to know how her class had fared under Marylou's tutelage.

But she shouldn't have worried.

"Hi, Teach," Marylou said when she saw Claire. "We're just about done here."

Claire looked around to see her students standing in line at the checkout, each of them pushing along a tray filled with fresh fruit, small boxes of whole-grain cereals, yogurt cups, small milk and orange juice cartons, and more.

"We all shopped," Marylou told her with some satisfaction. "We read labels, not that I understand them all that much, and we realized that if it comes with icing on it or inside it, it goes back on the shelf. Sort of hands-on experience, you know? And now they'll take home their class project—get it, class project?—and feed it all to their kids as their homework. My treat, Ruth is putting it all on one bill. I'm a genius, right?"

"You're Santa Claus without the suit," Chessie said, laughing. "But brilliant. Now come on. Class is letting out and I promised Nick we'd show up to watch Sean get his new belt or something before we go for that late dinner you promised me."

Claire tore her eyes away from the scene of her students all happily chattering as they loaded their "homework" into plastic bags Ruth had found somewhere, and looked up at the large clock on the wall. "You're coming, too? That's really very nice of you."

"Sean seemed upset that you might not be there to watch him," Chessie told her, "so I volunteered Marylou and myself. I'm actually looking forward to it. Do you think they'll break boards?"

"He said he does that sometimes. I don't know. He really was upset that I might not be there?"

"Father and son both," Chessie told her happily. "It's like I told you last night, you are probably worried for nothing. Kids know, that's what they always say. Kids and dogs. Does Nick have a dog?"

"No," Claire said, laughing, and then her heart leapt in her chest as she saw Nick sitting by himself on the bleachers. He saw her, and his smile as he stood up and waved her over had her heart skipping another beat. "But a dog would be nice, wouldn't it?"

"That's the way to think," Marylou said happily. "Stay positive. And don't tell me Nick's eyes don't get all gooey when he looks at you."

"Marylou, you're impossible," Claire whispered as they joined Nick. There was a small group of people sitting farther along the bleachers, but other than that, the gymnasium was empty. "Hi, sorry I'm late. Where's Sean?"

"He and Jacob will be marching in behind the instructors any moment now. I guess it's time for me to give the signal."

Before Claire could ask him what he meant, he stood up, put two fingers between his lips and gave a loud whistle.

Moments later, Salvatore and Evelina in the lead,

what seemed to be every student in Nick's class came marching into the gymnasium. They all carried signs that read: *Go, Sean! Go, Jacob!* Behind them, carrying their plastic bags filled with nutritious foods, came Claire's students, all of them laughing and talking as everyone climbed onto the bleachers before breaking into loud cheers as the small procession made its way to the center of the gymnasium floor.

"Look at him, look at him," Claire said, grabbing Nick's arm as Sean and Jacob waved to everyone. "Look at him *smiling*. Oh, Nick…"

"I nearly blew it, Claire," he told her quietly as everyone settled down and the Sensei motioned for the two boys to face him. With their arms close to their sides, their feet firmly together, both boys bowed to their teacher, and he to them. "I'd add it to my list of things to blame Sandy for, except that this wasn't her fault. I was so busy worrying about what might happen tomorrow that I forgot to pay attention to what's really important."

"Sean," Claire said, nodding.

Nick took her hand in his, squeezed it. "Not just Sean. Will you come back to the house with me tonight? Stay the night? Maybe talk about timelines?"

"Timelines? I don't understand."

"Neither did I, until Sean pointed out to me how there really aren't any that matter, not in some cases. Come home with me, and I'll try to explain."

"I have to work tomorrow, Nick. You don't want me to be there when—"

"This has nothing to do with Sandy. This has to do with you and me. If you agree that there is a you and me, could be a you and me."

Claire swallowed hard, ready to follow through on the only plan that had made sense to Marylou and Chessie and herself last night. The truth. "Yes. Because...because I—"

"Damn it! I forgot I have to videotape this thing," Nick interrupted, letting go of her hand and pulling his cell phone from his pocket, quickly opening and aiming it toward Sean, who had begun his testing.

...*love you*, Claire ended silently, smiling. *I really, really do.*

## Chapter Nine

"So, are you back in the running for father of the year?"

Nick handed Claire a glass of iced tea before he sat down on the side of the chaise where Claire was sitting, her long legs stretched out in front of her.

She'd followed him and Sean home after the ceremony, and they'd all celebrated with bowls of ice cream before the boy was sent off to shower and get ready for bed. Nick had just come back from saying goodnight to him.

"I was, until I nixed his idea that tomorrow should be designated a school holiday, to honor his achievement. I'll say this for the kid, he's always thinking. Are you warm enough?"

"I'm fine. It's so beautiful out here. Who takes care of the gardening?"

"Not me," he said, grinning at her in the light cast by solar lanterns spaced along the walkways and stairs, the soft glow of the strategically placed spotlights on the house itself, muted with the dimmer switch that could turn the yard from party time to romantic getaway. "My parents used to assign me yard work every year, and I'd moan and complain, even though I liked it. You don't want parents to know their plan is working, you know? But now I just don't have the time, so I hired a service. Do you like to garden?"

"I think I would. For now, I'm confined to pots on my balcony. I grew tomatoes there this summer, and actually harvested enough to make my own spaghetti sauce, and give some of the tomatoes away to my neighbors."

"And she cooks, too. A woman of many talents," he said, realizing that he had begun idly rubbing her bare leg. He slid his hand higher, underneath the hem of her skirt, held his palm still against her inner thigh. He liked touching her. It felt so natural to touch her. To have her in his life. He hadn't realized how busy his life had been, how fulfilled by having Sean in that life, yet how lonely he was at the same time. As a man.

"Nick."

"What? You want me to stop?"

"No—I mean yes. I can't stay the night," she told him, jackknifing to a sitting position beside him. "I wouldn't feel comfortable, not with Sean in the house. What if he woke up?"

Nick pulled her close, nuzzling her neck. "My son has been known to sleep through thunderstorms that rightly should have had him clinging to the ceiling by his fingernails. He won't wake up."

"He'll wake up tomorrow, for school. I can't be here when he does. It wouldn't be fair to him to possibly give him ideas about us that…you understand, don't you?"

"Yes." He put his hands on her shoulders and looked into her face, hoping, praying, he could find the right words. "Give him the idea that he's going to get what I never realized he wanted. A mother. I understand, Claire. And I know I'm probably going too fast for you. We both made one mistake we don't want to repeat, and we'd be idiots to rush into what might be another one."

She closed her eyes, nodded. "We've been… pretty intense. Maybe it's time we slowed things down a little. Got some perspective…"

"We could do that," Nick said, lightly rubbing her upper arms, because she may have said she wasn't cold, but she seemed to be shivering a little now. "The last thing I want is for you to feel there's any pressure on you."

She lifted her head, smiled at him. "Oh? So you haven't met Marylou and Chessie?"

"Chessie, too? How?"

Claire rolled her eyes. "You don't want to know. I mean, you really don't want to know."

He did his best to keep his voice light, teasing, as

he said, "Sean asked me how long it takes to know if you're in love."

"Oh, no. How did you answer him?"

"I said I'd get back to him."

"Chicken," Claire said, getting to her feet. Nick took her hand and they began walking slowly toward the house. "Is that why you mentioned timelines earlier tonight?"

"And now I'm thinking I shouldn't have. Because we're probably right to…to slow things down."

"It's the sensible thing to do. You've got a lot on your mind right now, what with your ex-wife coming back here, talking about being a mother to Sean again. And…and she left you. That's what you told me. So have you really had closure, Nick? Have you even seen her in the last six years?"

Her question surprised him into speaking before he thought. "And you left your ex-husband without confronting him. You just got on a plane and flew here to your brother. I mean," he added quickly, "I think, considering the circumstances, you were right to do what you did. But is that closure, Claire? Does it fit the definition as you're applying it to me?"

She stopped just before they reached the patio doors and turned to look at him.

"I never…I never thought about it that way. I never thought I had to confront Steven. I needed to confront myself, work my own way through what had happened, come to grips with the fact that, if Steven had made mistakes, so had I."

"I've had six years to do that, Claire," Nick told her, stepping closer to her, sliding his arms around her waist. "More, if I count the years we tried to pretend we hadn't made a mistake before Sandy did what we should have done much sooner. I don't know what she's doing now, why she's really coming here, but she's out of my life, and has been for a long time."

"She's still Sean's mother. You don't know how he's going to react when he sees her." Claire spread her hands against his chest. "Which is just another reason for me not to be here tomorrow morning. The only person you should be thinking about now is your son. That's your closure, Nick, seeing Sandy again, and the three of you deciding what her place is in your lives. And you're not there yet. Now, why don't you walk me to the door."

For now, he'd agree with her. For now, he'd let her walk away.

But only for now.

"I'll call you," he told her once she'd picked up her purse and sweater and they were outside once more, standing under the trellis with all its late-season blooms surrounding them with scent. He smiled as he stroked her cheek with his hand. She was still here, and yet he already missed her. "That's allowed, right?"

"Yes, please," she said, and then she turned her head and pressed a kiss into his palm. "I think we're doing the right thing, Nick. Even though it feels so very wrong."

He pulled her tight against him, capturing her mouth with his own, pouring all the unspoken words into his kiss, praying she knew that time apart would change nothing, Sandy's return would mean nothing. Claire clung to him, her fingertips digging into his back, giving him hope that she did know, that she felt the same way he did.

"Well, hello Nick. I thought about what my welcome would be like, but I've got to hand it to you. I didn't think about something like this."

Claire pushed away from him and turned around to face Sandy, even as she reached back, sought his hand and squeezed it tightly.

"Sandy," he said, looking at the woman he hadn't seen in six years, slightly taken aback to see her standing there, but that was all. Other than feeling irritation that she'd interrupted something wonderful between Claire and himself, he couldn't care less that she was back. "I thought you said you were coming tomorrow."

"I caught an earlier flight, thinking it might be fun to surprise you," she said, still looking at Claire. "Surprise!"

"I, um, I'd better get going," Claire said, trying unsuccessfully to free her hand from his grip. But he wasn't letting go.

"In a minute. Claire, this is Sean's mother, Sandy. Sandy, my friend, Claire Ayers."

"Cassandra," Sandy said, smiling brightly as she stuck out her right hand, pretty much leaving

Claire no choice but to take it. "Sorry to interrupt."

"That's quite all right, I was just leaving. A pleasure to meet you, Cassandra," Claire said before turning back to Nick. "I'll…I'll wait for your call. Tomorrow? Unless you're busy."

"Tomorrow," Nick told her, his hand at her back as he guided her past Sandy and, damn, her luggage. "Let me walk you to your car."

They walked the rest of the way in silence, Claire only speaking once she had opened her car door. "Well, that was uncomfortable, wasn't it? Did you see? She has her suitcases with her."

"I saw them, yes. Look, Claire—"

She put her fingers to his lips. "I tried to tell you something earlier tonight, Nick. Now I'm glad I didn't. Not because it wasn't true, isn't true. But if Sean should ever ask that question about time again, you can tell him that timing is everything. Tonight just wasn't the right time, for either of us."

He kissed her again, a quick, hard kiss, and then he let her go, watching until her taillights were out of sight around the bend before returning to the house. Sandy's suitcases were still on the path. But not Sandy.

He picked up the luggage and carried it inside the house.

"Tall, isn't she?" Sandy said as she stood in the foyer, applying lipstick in front of the mirror that hung there. "You always said you liked that I'm petite. I guess your tastes have changed?"

He looked at her as she continued to inspect her appearance in the mirror. She hadn't changed much in six years. Except, of course, for her name. And he felt nothing. Not love, not hate. Just…indifference. She could be a complete stranger, one he wasn't particularly interested in getting to know.

"You can't stay here, Sandy. I told you that when you called."

"Oh, for God's sake, Nick, lighten up, will you? It's nearly ten o'clock. They'll be rolling up the sidewalks here in domesticville in another ten minutes. Nobody's going to notice."

"Sean will notice when he wakes up tomorrow morning," Nick pointed out. "I haven't told him you were showing up."

She turned away from the mirror. "Really? Why not?"

"That should be obvious. I didn't know if you meant it."

"Oh? So now I don't say what I mean, is that it? When did I ever not do what I said I was going to do?"

Nick didn't know why he said it, but he heard himself saying, "You said until death do us part, *Cassandra*. That one, and the others. And we both know how that worked out."

Her bright smile was the old Sandy, as was her unaffected laugh. "I walked straight into that one, didn't I? Score one for Nick. Okay, you can drive me to a motel if it suits your prudish sense of decency. Happy now?"

"Not really, no. I can't leave Sean here alone."

"He's eight, Nick. You can leave him alone for the twenty minutes or so it would take to drive me to a motel."

"He's nine, and no, I can't. I'll call for a taxi."

"Suit yourself." Sandy flounced into the living room and sat down in one of the flowered couches, her feet dangling a few inches above the floor as the cushions tried to swallow her. "After all, we don't want to upset the girlfriend, do we?"

"Claire has nothing to do with whether or not I leave my son alone in—oh, forget it. I'll go look up the number of the cab service."

"And I'll try to claw my way out of this stupid couch," Sandy called after him. "I would have thought you'd have turned this place into a real bachelor's pad, Nicky. You know, a couple of those big wrap-around black leather couches, some chrome, maybe a bar over there in the corner. Oh, and…"

He ignored her as he opened a drawer in the kitchen and pulled out the telephone book, hoping the taxi service didn't quit at ten, proving Sandy's argument that Allentown might be growing, but it was still a long way from being her idea of Bright Lights, Big City.

"So you didn't tell him."

Sandy was standing behind him now, and Nick closed the telephone book and turned to look at her.

"No, I didn't. He has your photo next to his bed, Sandy. He knows who you are. I didn't want him to get his hopes up when he saw you. He'll think you're back to stay, and we both know that isn't true. You've had a disappointment, and you—"

"A *disappointment?* Is that what you call it, Nicky? Six years of my life, and he tosses me over for some, some—he had no right. *I* made him, Nicky. Me. My voice. My look. You just watch, he'll be back. *Begging.*"

"Keep your voice down," he told her. "Let me make some coffee."

"I don't want coffee," she said, heading for the far wall of cabinets. "You still keep the liquor in here? Yup, there it is. You're nothing if not dependable, Nick."

He watched as she found a glass and poured herself two inches of neat Scotch and then carried it over to the kitchen table. She sat down, sipped at the brown liquid, and then sighed. "Okay, that's better. I'm better. Can I see him?"

Nick was back to looking up the number for the taxi service. He hadn't known what he'd say if she asked him, not until he'd seen her, not until she'd said what she'd just said. "Sean? After what you said a minute ago? No. Absolutely not."

"I'm his mother."

"Not anymore. Not legally. You signed him away, just as you signed away our marriage. It's too late for you to come back and try to reclaim either. Because that's what this is all about, isn't it, Sandy? Waving Sean and me in front of Richie, making him sweat?

Get rid of the other singer, Richie, or I go back to Nick and our son? Let me guess. You told him where he could find you, didn't you? Luggage and all."

She didn't even bother to attempt looking embarrassed by her plan. "I sent him a text message, sure. He's got to figure out that he can't do this to me. Not now, and not ever again. He's got to see that I've got options, that I don't need him. It's just for a couple of days, Nicky. You can do this for a couple of days, can't you, help me out?"

"And Sean? What about him? Is he supposed to just be helping you out for a couple of days? That's how you're seeing this whole thing?"

"That's different. He'll want to see me, and once I started thinking about it, I knew I wanted to see him. I'm his mother, and I've got maternal feelings just like any mother. You said it, Nicky, he's got my photo next to his bed. Or do you want to wait until he's grown up and I tell him you kept me away from him for years and years, deliberately turned him against me? How do you think he'd react to that? A couple of days, and I'll be gone. Or we can play hardball."

"Using your own son," Nick said in disgust. Yet he knew he was powerless in this one. Sean had always been curious about his mother. How could he deny the boy the chance, perhaps the only chance he'd ever have, of seeing her?

"I told you, Nick, that's your decision, not mine. Do this, and I'll go away, never bother you again.

And I'll be better at this mom thing. I'll send post-cards, and gifts and stuff. Call him once in a while now that he's old enough to hold a conversation— nine is old enough for that, right? I promise, I'll do all of that. But if you won't help me? Hey, maybe then I'll have no choice but to stay here in Dulltown, forever, and forget Vegas. There's that new casino over in Bethlehem. I shouldn't have much trouble finding a band, getting a gig going there. Pennsyl-vania is loaded with casinos now, and the Jersey shore, and all of those casinos. Live entertainment, Nick, they're all doing it. Vegas isn't everything."

Nick closed the telephone book and slid it back in the drawer. "Monday. You can stay for the weekend, but then that's it, Richie or no Richie. That's the offer, Sandy, and then you're gone."

"Monday? That's cutting it close. But Richie should be here by then, begging me to come back. He never thought I'd do it, pack up and leave. But I've called his bluff. All right. It's a deal."

"Lucky me," Nick mumbled under his breath. "I'll put you in the downstairs guest room. And you stay there quietly until I get Sean off to school tomorrow. I'll prepare him on the way home after classes and his basketball game."

"Prepare him? Anyone would think you're going to give him bad news."

Nick opened his mouth to give her an answer to that one, but then changed his mind. They might have several battles ahead of them in the next few days. He should save his ammunition. "I'll get some sheets from the linen closet and you can make up the bed."

When she hadn't heard from Nick by noon, Claire worried that her cell phone battery had gone dead. But it hadn't. She checked to make sure she had the thing on vibrate, as she was hiding it in the pocket of her exam coat, and had not turned off the ringer by mistake. She hadn't.

But then one of the nurses had told everyone that one of the parents had been late for her son's post-ear infection checkup appointment because of some sort of situation at the courthouse that was playing out right now on local television.

"Some guy appearing in domestic court or whatever it's called pulled a gun and is threatening to blow his brains out if he can't see his kids," the nurse informed her. "Like that's going to help his case, right? Anyway, the mom got all caught up in watching the live report, and almost forgot the appointment."

Hearing the news, Claire decided that Nick was probably at the courthouse with all the other reporters, and was too busy to phone her.

So she relaxed. Sort of.

He'd call. As soon as he had time, he'd call her.

By four o'clock the suicidal guy had long since been talked into turning over his weapon, and still Nick had not called her.

A little before six, Claire was sitting in Chessie

Burton's living room above Second Chance Bridal after the two shared some Chinese take-out, telling her everything that had happened the previous evening.

"Naturally, she's gorgeous," she told her new friend as Chessie handed her a tall glass of iced tea. "She looks like all those little blondes from the exercise class at the community center—but with better makeup. I felt like a giant, standing next to her. I don't know if she's a natural blonde, but that doesn't matter, does it? And she's got this husky sort of voice, and she had a bunch of suitcases with her, and—"

"Would you just listen to you?" Chessie interrupted, laughing. "A skinny shrimp of a dyed blonde wearing tons of makeup and with a smoker's rasp shows up, and you call that competition? Get real."

"I know, none of that matters. What matters is that Nick was married to her, that she gave him a son, and that she walked out on him. He didn't leave her, they didn't decide to divorce. She left him flat."

"She left him with a three-year-old to raise, Claire. So she could be a rock star? Yes, I can see why Nick would welcome her back with open arms, forgive her everything. Are you nuts?"

This was why Claire had come to Second Chance Bridal. She knew Chessie Burton was the sort of person who cut directly to the chase, said what was on her mind. She needed that right now.

"I know, he has every reason to hate her, actually.

But she is Sean's mother. People grow up, Chessie. She might deeply regret what she did six years ago. If there's any chance that she did, that she wants a second chance with Sean, how can Nick refuse to let her back into their son's life?"

"Leaving you...where?" Chessie prodded. "Because now I think we're getting to the heart of this thing."

Claire put down her glass, the contents untouched. "I'm that obvious?"

"That maybe you've been weaving little fantasies of you and Nick and Sean being a family? You told me about the house, which sounds like something out of a fairy tale. You love Nick, we've established that, or at least I have. I can see you're still second-guessing yourself, probably because everything has been moving pretty fast. You love Sean, and who wouldn't, he's a sweetheart. Marylou was looking like a genius—and you didn't hear me say that one! And then, bam, just as the fairy tale is about to get to the happily ever after part, along comes the witch. Don't you just hate it when that happens?"

Claire laughed in spite of herself. But then she sobered. "So, Chessie, am I in love with Nick, or the fairy tale?"

"Oh no, I'm not going there. Only you can answer that question, babe."

"And I don't blame you. You know, maybe Sandy showing up right now is a good thing."

"Really? Okay, Pollyanna, explain that one. Because I'm really not seeing it."

"Sean wants a mother. I don't think I'm so wonderful that he just instantly fell in love with me. He's probably been looking for a mother for a long time, the poor kid, and I just happen to be the person who showed up. So, thinking that way, it's also the perfect time for Sandy to show up. Because he has to be wondering where she is, why she left him. Now, in a way, he'll have a choice. I mean, if Nick and I...you know."

"You really think Sean would see it that way? Either-or? Daddy and Claire, or Mommy? That's a little heavy for a nine-year-old, don't you think?"

Claire shook her head. "Obviously you aren't around children very much. They may not be emotionally mature enough to really sort through heavy thinking like that, but that doesn't mean they don't think it. They can be very black and white, with no shades of gray. They're also the wisest creatures on earth when it comes to sensing who loves them and who doesn't. Not that Nick should be worried for himself, and I hope he isn't. He's been both mother and father to Sean for as long as the child can remember. But then again, Sandy's got the added bonus of being the glamorous mommy dropping out of the sky."

Chessie leaned back on the couch cushions and stared at Claire. "Wait a minute. I thought you were thinking about Sandy and you. Comparison mommy shopping, you know? But when we get right down to the nitty-gritty here, you're worried about *Nick*? Sean choosing Sandy over Nick? Well, that settles that one, doesn't it? Now I will answer you. You love him."

Claire considered this for some moments, and then smiled, even as her eyes stung with tears. "Yes. I guess I do, don't I? Now, tell me what it means that I think I'm going to kill him if he doesn't call me soon?"

"Dad?"

Nick looked up from the computer screen. He'd filed his story on the courthouse standoff hours ago, but that hadn't kept him from reading over the copy again, just to satisfy himself that he'd stuck to the facts and not injected any opinion into the piece. In a few days, if the guy was released from his mandatory seventy-two-hour psych hospitalization, he might be able to interview him, as a follow-up to his series.

"Yeah, Slugger?" He closed the laptop and patted the chaise cushion, inviting his son to sit down beside him. "How's it going in there?"

"Okay, I guess."

"You guess? You want to talk about it?"

Sean shot a look toward the patio doors. "She looks just like the picture in my room, doesn't she?"

Sandy's looks hadn't been Nick's first choice of topic, but he'd let Sean ease his way into whatever it was he wanted to say. "You have her same color hair. I know it doesn't look it, but ladies like to make their hair different colors sometimes. And her nose.

You've got your mother's nose. You should probably thank her for that," he said with a smile as he touched a fingertip to the bump on his own nose.

"Uh-huh. But I'm tall, like you. I'm almost as tall as her. So that's okay."

Nick had a million questions he longed to ask, but decided to let Sean guide him. Which meant that neither of them said anything for several minutes.

It hadn't been easy, telling Sean that his mother was in town and wanted to see him. He'd waited until after the basketball game, not wanting to put anything too heavy on him until then, and then had broken the news over hotdogs and fries at Sean's favorite shop. He could eat a double helping of vegetables tomorrow.

Sean hadn't reacted in any of the many ways Nick might have supposed. He'd just nodded, said, "Okay," and that had been the end of it. Sandy had been waiting in the foyer when they walked into the house, ready to swoop Sean into a hug, but Sean had stayed fairly stiff in her embrace.

That, as Claire had said last night, had been *uncomfortable*.

Sandy had asked what they should do for dinner—another uncomfortable moment. She looked as if she might snipe at him for not considering her, but she'd managed to force a smile and say it didn't matter, she wasn't hungry anyway…she just wanted to see her baby.

*Baby. Not a great choice of words, Sandy,* Nick knew.

Part of him had wanted to stay close to Sean, act as a buffer or whatever, but another part of him knew that this first meeting was something Sandy and Sean had to handle between them. After about a half hour, he'd suggested that Sean take Sandy to his room, to show her his basketball and karate trophies, and then come out onto the patio to try to lose himself on the Internet.

Now a full hour had passed, and all Sean had to say was "Okay, I guess."

"She didn't know what grade I'm in," Sean said now.

"She hasn't been here, Slugger. It's understandable."

"She said I should be in your old bedroom, the one upstairs over the garage. She said you used to sneak out at night. Did you used to do that, Dad? Is that why I'm still in the baby room next to yours?"

Nice. Sandy had been in the house less than twenty-four hours, and she was trying to undermine him as Sean's father. "My old room is clear on the other side of the house. I'd rather have you near me."

Sean nodded. "But can I have that room when I'm older?"

"Sure," Nick told him. "Right after I find the key for the deadbolt and hide it somewhere."

Sean smiled at that, but it was a small smile. "Where was she, Dad? I asked her, but she just said she was lots of places, and that's why she didn't take me with her, and so that's why she made you keep me."

Nick felt his hands drawing up into fists and consciously relaxed his fingers. "Your mother didn't *make* me do anything, Sean. You're here, the two of us are here, because you're my son, and I love you more than anything or anyone else in this world. You...you must have misunderstood your mother."

There, he'd been charitable. He'd given an excuse for how Sandy had been trying to make herself look good and him look bad. Damn her.

"Okay. Was she in jail?"

Nick gave an involuntary bark of laughter at the question. You could read all the books, listen to all the experts—but nobody could really figure out how a child's mind works.

"No, Sean, your mother wasn't in jail. She sings with a band, remember? Bands travel a lot."

"So she'll be leaving soon? To travel?"

Nick heard the hope in his son's voice, and for a moment, actually felt bad for Sandy. She'd gone hunting everywhere for fulfillment, and now she'd lost the only thing that could ever have any lasting meaning: the unquestioning love of her own child.

"Is that what you want, Sean?" he asked his son, realizing that he had only referred to his mother as *she* this whole time, and never *Mom*, or *Mommy*.

"We're supposed to go to the movies tomorrow, with Miss Ayers. Remember, Dad?"

"Yes, I remember. But that was before your mother...arrived."

"Oh, she doesn't want to go. I asked her. She said

she wants to stay here to wait for somebody who'd better show up if he knows what's good for him."

There was something else Sandy hadn't learned, thanks to her absence. Kids remember everything you don't want them to remember, and repeat most of it word-for-damning-word when you'd least like them to.

"But then I guess Miss Ayers wouldn't want to come back here with us anyway, not if she's here."

"Why would you think that, Champ?"

Sean rolled his eyes. "Da-ad, you were kissing Miss Ayers the other night, remember? She might get mad if she knew that…that *she* was here." He got to his feet, looking at his father as if he worried for his sanity. "We like Miss Ayers. You don't want to mess this up, Dad."

Nick opened his arms to his son. "Come here," he said, gathering Sean into a hug, kissing his hair. "You're something else, Champ, you know that?"

Sean returned the hug, holding on tight for a few moments, but then pushed himself free. "So I can go play video games in my room now? I don't have to talk to her anymore?"

"Sean, she is your mother. You have to at least give her a chance."

"I suppose," he said, his slim shoulders slumping. "But I don't think she cares all that much. She was on her phone when I came out here, and it was like she just wanted me out of the room."

Nick got to his feet, his heartbeat accelerating. "On the phone?"

"Yeah, somebody called Richie. She just pushed me out of the den and closed the door. I'm not dumb, Dad. She doesn't want to be here. So why should I want her here?"

Finally, Nick got what he thought he would get from Sean, even as he dreaded seeing his son upset. He pulled him onto his lap and held him as he had when he was a baby, and let him cry.

## Chapter Ten

Claire toed the door shut behind her and quickly placed the pair of grocery bags on the bar before grabbing up the phone. "Hello?"

"I was about to hang up. Did I get you out of the shower—and let us both pause now for a moment while I hold on to the mental image I've just conjured up."

She subsided onto one of the bar stools, ridiculously pleased to hear his voice. "Hello, Nick," she said, smiling. "How's it going? How's Sean?"

"Better, I think," he said, his voice no longer teasing. "I sent him back to school today, and he says he wants to go to karate tonight. He asked me if you'd be there."

"He did?" Her heart skipped a beat. She really

wanted to see Sean, to see Nick, but this first meeting since Sandy had come to town—and almost just as quickly disappeared again—could be awkward. Not to mention complicated.

"I nearly told him he'd have to get in line, but I restrained myself. You do know that it has been four days, sixteen hours and…twenty-seven minutes since I've kissed you?"

"It was better that way."

"Speak for yourself, Ms. Ayers," he said, but again, there was no teasing in his voice. "He's not latching onto you, Claire. He's not making a choice, either. Sandy is Sandy, and you're you. She promised she'd call him, keep in contact, but he told me she won't. Broke my heart to hear him say that, but if that's how he wants to handle it, I can't stop him. He doesn't want to get hurt again."

"I can't blame him for that," Claire said as she got up from the stool and began emptying the grocery bags, shoved a pack of hamburger in the refrigerator. She had to keep moving or else she'd be late for class. "I can't just waltz in and take Sandy's place, either. I mean, not that I'm saying that I expect to just…I mean, we haven't really discussed…I'm not presuming…and it really isn't good to have women just coming and going around your son, Nick…not that you'd ever do anything like—can we talk about this later?"

God. Could she have sounded more ridiculous? They liked each other, they'd been to bed together.

Twenty years ago, that was almost as good as a proposal. Now it was just being *adult*.

Except it was so much more. For her, definitely. For him, she hoped so. It was the timing. Thanks to Sandy, it was all in the damn *timing*. Were four days, sixteen hours and now thirty minutes enough time?

"I think we'd better, yes," he said quietly. "Unless you're still feeling uncomfortable about..."

"I'm not uncomfortable, Nick," she said, blinking back sudden tears. "I'm trying—we're trying—to be adults about this thing." She winced at her use of *adult*. "Sean has to come first right now, and he's had a rough few days. Oh, darn it, there goes my cell. I've got a text coming in. Hang on a sec, okay?"

She grabbed her cell out of her purse and read the message: *Skl bus kids LVH ER asap D.*

*On my way* she texted back and picked up her house phone once more.

"Nick? Is Sean home yet?"

"Yeah, why? What's up?"

"Okay, that's one worry gone. That was Derek. It looks like there's been a school bus accident, and he needs me at Lehigh Valley Hospital. I've got to go."

"Yes, of course. I just got a beep, myself. Probably Fred. Do you want me to call the community center? No, wait, nobody's there yet. I'll call Marylou, tell her neither of us can make it tonight."

"What about Sean?" Claire was already tossing butter and milk into the refrigerator and grabbing two slices of bread and some slices of boiled ham out of the meat drawer, slamming it all together in a dry sandwich she'd take with her, eat on the way.

Nick swore under his breath. "Mrs. Nicholson is still on vacation. I don't know what I'll do with—don't worry about that. You're needed at the hospital. I'll take care of things at this end. Call me on my cell if you can get away to the cafeteria at some point."

Not a single word about how much easier it would be if she went to Sean while he went to work writing up the news on the crash. No recriminations about how her insistence on a career was eating into their personal lives. Just *you're needed at the hospital*. He couldn't know how much she loved him at this moment.

"I'll do that, I promise," Claire agreed and hung up the phone, already grabbing for her purse and car keys. Kids, riding in a school bus. No restraints because—no, she'd never been able to see the logic in strapping children into car seats and boosters in family cars, but letting them ride without restraints on buses, where an accident could have them flying around the interior of the bus like leaves in a windstorm.

"Head and facial injuries, lost teeth, broken bones," she mumbled to herself as she drove, her mind operating objectively, assessing what she might encounter, how she would assist Derek in any way she could. She switched on the radio to listen for news bulletins, and soon learned that the bus was on its way through the area, and heading back to a suburban Philadelphia school after a day trip to New York. Several injuries, none life-threatening—which she knew didn't rhyme with *slap on a bandage and send them home*.

She took alternate routes through Allentown, having learned that the accident had closed the thruway, her usual route, and arrived just ahead of an emergency vehicle that swung into the ambulance bay, where three other ambulances were already unloading patients. No wonder Derek had been called in to help.

It was after ten by the time she'd written up the admitting papers for the third child needing further care, and spoken with parents who had driven to the hospital to be with their children. She'd heard a few of the ambulance drivers and EMTs talking about the scene, and it seemed a miracle that none of the children were more seriously hurt.

"How are we doing?" Derek asked her as she pulled down a set of x-rays showing several broken teeth and a dislocated jaw and replaced them in their folder.

"That depends. You have anything else for me? You were great, by the way. Kids adore you. How many exam-glove balloons did you blow up tonight?"

"I lost count. One of them insisted on two, because he had two stitches. I was beginning to see spots before my eyes before I got out of there. Hey, go home. You look beat."

"Does that mean I have tomorrow morning off, boss?" she asked him, earning herself a kiss on the cheek and an *in your dreams, sis* before her cell phone began to vibrate in her exam coat pocket.

It had to be Nick. Maybe he was already waiting for her in the hospital cafeteria. It seemed like years she'd talked to him. Longer since she'd seen him, other than in those dreams Derek had mentioned.

She left the emergency unit and found a quiet spot in the hall before opening her phone, to see that she didn't recognize the number displayed on the screen. "Hello?"

"Claire Ayers?"

"Yes," Claire said cautiously, not recognizing the voice. Or maybe she did, but didn't want to acknowledge that she did. "Who is this, please?"

"Cassandra Barrington. Well, not really. I changed it, legally. I'm Cassandra Starr now. Two R's."

"Ms. Starr," Claire said, feeling ridiculous. "How…how did you get my number?"

"Oh, that's easy. I snoop," Sandy answered with a laugh. "I'm really good at it, too. Nick's got condoms in his nightstand, and it looks like a pretty new box, only a couple missing. Good for him. Good for you."

Claire sagged against the wall. "I'm going to hang up now."

"No! I shouldn't have said that. I'm sorry. Look, don't you want to know why I'm calling you?"

"I don't think so, no."

"I want to talk to you about Sean. My son."

Claire's heart rate nearly doubled. "All right, I'm listening."

"I don't know how to say this, Claire," Cassandra went on, her slightly raspy voice breaking slightly.

as if she might be fighting tears. "I…I stink as a mother. I came to Allentown to screw with Richie's head, and I ended up making my own kid cry. I feel like crap, Claire, you know? He's a cute kid, really smart. He looked me square in the eye on Sunday morning and told me he knew he couldn't count on me, but that was all right because he had Nick. And you."

Claire pressed her fist to her mouth and turned her back as two nurses walked past, so that they wouldn't see her expression and think something was wrong. She prayed nothing was wrong. "I…I see."

"Do you? Do you know what it's like to feel a knife plunged into your heart, and then twisted?"

"You didn't have to leave," Claire pointed out, trying very hard not to feel sorry for this woman. "Sean needs a mother. He deserves a mother."

"Yes, a mother. Not me, not *his* mother. A mother. I can't be what he needs. I think…I don't know, maybe I'm missing a gene or something. I love him, but I'd only end up screwing him up if I gave up my career for him, you know? I'd resent it. Hell, I resent that I'm sitting here in Vegas, crying like a baby over a kid who doesn't even like me."

"I'm sorry, Cassandra."

"Yeah, me too. But here's what I want to know. I couldn't get spit out of Nick when I asked him, so I'm coming straight to you. Is Sean right?"

Claire tried to swallow, but her mouth had gone dry. "Is he right about what?"

"About what? For crying out loud, do I have to draw you a picture? About you and Nick. I know Nick loves you. He nearly jumped down my throat when I brought up your name. He's very protective. I know Sean loves…is crazy about you. What I don't know, Claire, is how you feel. I need to know that."

"If you don't mind, Cassandra, I think Nick should be the first person who hears how I feel about him."

There was a short bark of laughter at the other end of the phone. "Okay, good one. But I think I get the drift. So here's the deal. I screwed up, I admit that. I screwed up by staying away, and I screwed up by showing up. But I made a promise to Sean before I left, and I intend to keep it, even if he doesn't believe me. I'm not going to disappear again. But I want you to know that I'm not going to get in your way, either. Kids need to know they're secure, right? Nick's his security, and you, too, I'm guessing. I won't mess with that. But, please, don't shut me out of my son's life. We can, you know, e-mail each other, stuff like that? You could keep me up to date, kick me in the backside if I haven't called at least twice a month. Like that?"

Claire realized that if she agreed, it was as good as saying yes to Nick if he showed up in the cafeteria, got down on one knee, and asked her to marry him. Strange that she would make her first commitment to Nick's ex-wife.

"Yes, we can do that, Cassandra," she said,

taking the first step in the direction her heart knew almost from the first that she should go. "I'm sure Nick will agree."

"Maybe. Only if he thinks I won't be a bad influence on Sean," Sandy said, and then sighed. "I'm hoping you'll convince him."

"Cassandra, Sean cried for two days when you left. Nick knows a child will always love his mother. That's simply the way it is. I'm just so happy that you're going to be a larger part of his life."

"But never the most important part," Sandy said, sighing. "You know, the part that helps him with his homework or teaches him how to dance before his first…his first date. Damn, here I go again, getting all weepy. Richie thinks I'm nuts. Let me just hang up for now, okay? Nick has my e-mail address now, so if he agrees, you can get it from him. And I'll answer, I promise."

"I'll do the best I can, Cassandra. And thank you."

"Uh-huh, sure. But you know how you can thank me? You can make Nick get rid of those damn flowered couches. Bye!"

Claire closed her phone, and smiled as she stuck it back in her pocket, only to have it begin vibrating with another call.

This time it had to be Nick. She quickly fished the phone out of her pocket and put it to her ear. "Hello? Nick?"

"Claire? Hi, it's me, Marylou. Sorry I'm not Nick, but I was just wondering when you guys thought you might get home. Sean's been asleep for a couple of hours now, and I'm starting to dream about my own mattress. Not that I mind!"

Claire headed back into the unit, so that she could get to the cafeteria without having to walk all the way around the outside of the huge building. "Nick got *you* to babysit?"

"You say that as if I don't know how to do it. And he didn't get me to babysit. I volunteered. He found one of the *Chronicle's* reporters to take over his class and I took Sean to his class and then subbed for you again."

"You're a lifesaver, Marylou, thank you. But I didn't fax over a lesson plan," Claire said, wondering if Marylou might be eligible for a Nobel Prize or something.

"Just remembered that, did you? It was okay. Chessie had a late appointment, meaning I couldn't snag her to babysit again, so we used little Stefano to show how to properly bathe an infant. Let me tell you, Claire, that baby has quite a set of lungs on him."

"Didn't like his bath, huh?" Claire asked as she pushed through a set of fire doors and entered the main lobby, looking around her, hoping to see Nick.

"As the kids say, not hardly. Claire?"

"I'm looking for Nick now. Why didn't you just call him? Well, never mind, I'll find him for you."

"That's what I'm trying to tell you. I know I could have called Nick, but I really wanted to talk to you," Marylou said, her voice dropping as if she might be overheard. "Chessie didn't really have a late appointment tonight."

Claire stopped walking and went to the side of the corridor, the better to hear Marylou. "Okay. What's wrong?"

"I'll tell you this much, that woman can be *so* glad I wasn't there when Chessie ran into her today at the mall around lunchtime. Chessie was there picking up a little engraved gift for Barb for Saturday. She does that, you know, gives each bride a little engraved gift. She's such a sweetheart, isn't—"

"Marylou, I'm trying to find Nick for you. You want to speed this up a little? What woman should be glad?"

"Diana Peters, aka Chessie's maid of honor, aka the bimbo who took off with the groom five years ago, the night before the wedding."

"Oh, that's not good, is it? But Chessie's over that, she said so."

"Anyone can talk a good story, Claire. And maybe it's true, too. But that doesn't mean you can have your former best friend tell you to your face that she and that rotten Rick Peters are divorcing and— Chessie says this is word-for-word—*I'm done with him, so you can have him back now.* And then she said she'd be sure to tell Rick he should call her, so they could catch up on *old times*."

"Oh, poor Chessie. You don't want to go home, do you, Marylou? You're going over to Second

Chance Bridal, to see her. Look, if I can't find Nick, I'll be right there, so you can leave. Give me fifteen minutes, okay?"

Nick pulled into the driveway and parked beside Claire's car. He hadn't planned it this way, but she was here, and he was here, and after four long days and nights of not seeing her, he figured he could confine himself to *grateful* and not look too hard at the *why* of it.

He'd been at the State Police barracks when Claire phoned him, pulling together the facts surrounding the accident, and the charges being brought against the driver of a tractor trailer that had sideswiped the school bus as he merged onto the highway.

Once he knew Claire was on her way to relieve Marylou, Nick drove to the office to write his story, as deadline was fast approaching and he wanted to do two sidebars—one about one of the children who was injured, and another on the continuing battle to make belt restraints mandatory in any vehicle transporting children. He'd gotten that idea from Claire, who'd complained to him that nearly all of the injuries could have been avoided if the students had been restrained.

He'd teased her that she was fast becoming his muse, if not his editor, but he genuinely enjoyed her lively mind, her ideas. She wasn't just another pretty face, not Claire. He was still trying to figure out how he'd gotten so lucky.

But tonight would have nothing to do with luck. She'd either want him or she wouldn't.

Nick entered the quiet house just as the mantel clock in the living room chimed out the hour of midnight, and softly called Claire's name. There was no answer.

He checked the kitchen, the den—took a shot and tried his bedroom—before peeking into Sean's room to see his son sound asleep on his back on top of the covers, his arms and legs splayed out as if he was trying to turn his body into the letter X.

Nick had read somewhere that the position a sleeper assumes shows a lot about his mental state. Sean had spent the last few nights pretty much drawn up into a fetal position in his bed, as if protecting himself from some unseen assault. Sleeping on one's back, Nick remembered, showed a mind at peace, a confident person willing to open himself up to the world.

The photograph of his mother, which had been banished to the bottom of his closet, was once again on the nightstand beside him. Nick couldn't be sure, but he had a pretty good idea who had brought about that change, when he had been unable to get through to his son.

Sometimes being a parent broke your heart in a bad way…and sometimes it broke your heart in a good way. Nick went into the room and bent over Sean, placing a light kiss on the boy's soft cheek. Tonight it was in a good way.

Stripping off his tie and unbuttoning his shirt as he returned to his own bedroom, Nick quickly changed into a favorite worn Lehigh University T-shirt and a pair of sweats, and went hunting Claire once more.

He found her in the living room, curled up on her side on one of the floral couches, a mohair throw his mother had crocheted draped over her as she slept.

Her hair was loose and falling over her face, one hand tucked under her cheek.

"Hey, sleepyhead," he said, perching himself on the edge of the cushions and pushing the hair back from her face so that he could press a light kiss against her ear. "I'm sorry I'm so late."

Claire slowly opened her eyes, turning onto her back to smile up at him. "Don't apologize. I think I needed that nap. I really have to ask Sean to show me how to work your TV remote." She motioned for him to move and sat up. "What time is it, anyway?"

"A little after midnight," he told her, watching her stretch like a cat just waking from a nap. It was all he could do to keep his hands off her.

She pushed herself to her feet. "I'll make some coffee. I'll need it for the drive home. And I did want to talk to you some more about Cassandra's phone call."

Nick followed her into the kitchen. "She really got to you, didn't she?"

Claire pressed the button on the coffee machine, obviously having already filled and programmed it. "She got to you, once. You loved her, remember?"

He knew himself to be on treacherous ground now, and decided to stick with the truth. That was the only thing that really worked long-term, anyway. "Yes, I loved her. She was exciting, different." He smiled at a sudden memory. "When I first saw her on campus, she was wearing one of those granny dresses or whatever they're called, and she had hair hanging halfway down her back. Brown hair, by the way. She carried an acoustic guitar with her, strapped on her back, even to classes. That didn't last long."

"The granny dresses or the classes?" Claire asked him as she got out cups and a bag of sugar cookies.

"Both. Sandy was an English major, but she dropped out a few months after we started dating, only one semester away from her degree. She'd found a band and the folk singer dresses went, the hair changed colors—pink the first time—and the acoustic guitar was traded in for a secondhand electric. Also pink." His smile faded. "And I started backing away, a move I don't know if she even noticed, because she was so caught up with the band. Then the test strip turned blue or whatever those things do, and that was that. I guess you'd say that's the abbreviated version, but yes, I loved her. I think I did. Then, for a long time, I hated her."

Claire poured the coffee and carried the mugs to the kitchen table. "That's only natural. She left you. She left Sean."

"I suppose so. Now? Now, I don't really feel anything for her. That surprised me this weekend. When it comes to Sandy now, I guess I'm Switzerland. Completely neutral. Except that I do feel sorry for her. She's going to spend her life chasing a dream."

"I'm no huge expert on this sort of thing, Nick," Claire said after a moment. "But I think you've just described closure. How does it feel?"

He laughed softly under his breath, and thought about her question. "Different. Good. Mostly, it feels good. Sean's all right, better than I could have expected. He's one hell of a kid. Not that he wasn't rocky there for a few days, but we're moving through it. I saw Sandy's picture is back on his nightstand."

"We…talked a bit, and he decided to put it back."

Nick lifted her hand to his mouth, kissed the soft skin of her palm. "I've missed you. Are we done with our slowing it down experiment now? Are we ready for the next step?"

She dipped her head for a moment. When she looked up at him again he thought he had his answer. And then she surprised him. "Possibly. Maybe."

"Excuse me?" Was she going to say they were still moving too fast? Was she going to tell him that she wasn't ready to take on a man with a nine-year-old son, no matter how cute Sean was and how much she liked him? Did she look at him and think he was still carrying too much baggage?

"Claire, you were right. There are things about me this week that weren't there last week. But that doesn't mean that anything has changed in my feelings for you. But now it sounds as if you're saying—"

She waved a hand in front of him, signaling that she wanted to talk. "I'm not, Nick. Really, I'm not. It's just that I think maybe, before we say anything else, we should…practice some more." Now her brown eyes were twinkling.

He relaxed against the back of the chair. "Practice. Really?"

"Yes. Before we make a commitment, you know?"

"Claire Ayers, are you asking me to take you to bed? Why, I'm shocked."

"No, you're not," she told him, getting to her feet, pulling her up with him.

"You're right, I'm not. In fact, taking you to bed has been on my mind all day today, so I'm glad we're not going to talk anymore tonight. We've probably had enough talking, enough thinking for a while," he said, drawing her down the hallway toward his bedroom, stopping just inside the doorway. "But I'm still going to ask you, you know. Sooner or later."

"Um-hum, you do that," Claire said, just before she shut the door, put both hands against his chest and began pushing him backwards, toward the bed. "And sooner or later, I'll answer you. Just not tonight. Do you mind?"

He had already finished unbuttoning her blouse and had moved on to the front closure of her bra. "I think I can find a way to manage my disappoint-ment," he told her as the clasp came undone and he cupped her breasts in his hands. He stroked his thumbs over her nipples, feeling them stiffen at his touch. "How about you?"

"Nick...you're still talking..."

She was right. So he kissed her instead. Tasted her sweetness. Thrilled to her hunger. Felt his breath catch in his throat as she reached down her hand and slid it inside the waistband of his shorts.

He loved this woman. She was everything he'd ever wanted, everything he'd ever needed. She knew when to hold back, and she knew when to take what she wanted.

Tonight, he would give her everything he had to give. And then he'd give her more...

Claire cried at Barb and Skip's wedding. She didn't really know either one of them, but she'd cried anyway, because the ceremony was so beautiful, Barb and Skip were so beautiful, their love so great it was tangible for anyone who cared to look at them.

Sean had looked over at her at one point and laughed, telling Nick about her tears once the ceremony was over, laughing again in the telling, as if he'd never seen anything quite so funny. "Claire said she was crying because she was happy, Dad. Boys don't do that. Are we going to eat soon?"

"So much for hoping my son has any romance in his soul," Nick joked as they made their way out of the Rose Gardens and back to his car. "And don't touch that bow tie, Sean. It has to stay on until we're done with all the photographs, okay? And that's not just me saying it. Your cousin Barb gave me strict orders."

"Oh, man…"

Claire laughed as Sean climbed into the back seat, loving the exchange between father and son, loving how right it all seemed to be here with the two of them. Sean had, with his father's permission, begun calling her Claire, and she liked that, too. Every day was a step forward now, and each step seemed surer than the last.

At the reception, Nick introduced her to his parents and his sister, and that was another step forward. They all sat together and the conversation flowed naturally. Annie Barrington seemed especially pleased to hear Claire's opinion of her former kitchen, but then leaned closer to confide quietly, "But I do think the appliances could do with a little updating, don't you? Sometimes I think Nick believes he's living in a museum, and nothing can change, or else I'll be offended. He's also been very busy, raising Sean, but it's time he put his own stamp on the house, makes it a home for his family, begin his own traditions. You'll help him with that, won't you, dear?"

Claire had smiled politely and mumbled something she'd hoped was appropriate, but she knew she had just gotten the seal of approval from Nick's parents.

Another step forward.

Tonight, she'd tell Nick she loved him. He had to know, but she still hadn't said the words she'd nearly blurted out much too soon; the same words he'd nearly said too soon. Now, the time was right.

"What are you smiling about?"

Claire turned in her chair to look at Nick, who had come up behind her without her noticing. "Nothing. I was just thinking about your parents, and how they're taking Sean for the night so he can swim in the hotel pool. That's all."

"That's all? You're not thinking that we'll be alone tonight, and that maybe something…special might happen tonight? I did tell you I was going to ask you again, remember."

"And you still think I'm being silly."

Nick went down on one knee beside her, so that she looked nervously toward his parents, who were still sitting at the table. "No, I think you're wise, and wonderful, and even if many would still say we're rushing things, I think we both know what we want, and know that it's right. In fact, you've been right about everything, Claire, except for one thing in our timeline. You're off by about five hours, as a matter of fact."

Claire shot a quick look toward his family and then tugged at his sleeve, trying to get him to stand up, because not only was his family watching and listening, but it seemed as if the whole room was silent, straining to hear his every word. "Nick, please. Get up."

"Nope," he said, taking her hands in his. "But you might want to look behind you, sweetheart, because a few more guests have arrived."

"What are you talking—Mom? Dad?" Claire couldn't believe it. Not only were her parents standing there when they should be in Chicago, but Derek and his wife and children as well. She turned back to Nick and whispered fiercely, "What did you do?"

"It's pretty obvious, isn't it?" he whispered back to her. "I took the next step. Besides, I wanted to ask your parents' permission, and when I called, well, one thing sort of led to the next, and they thought a visit to their grandchildren was in order." And then he reached into his pocket and pulled out a small velvet box and opened it, revealing the most beautiful diamond ring she'd ever seen. "Claire, I love you. I've loved you almost from the moment we met, and I will love you until the day I die."

"I love you, too," she said quietly, feeling every eye on her, but seeing only Nick.

"Just *ask* her, Dad," came an exasperated voice, and everyone laughed as Sean's ears turned rather red and he buried his face against his grandfather's chest.

"Thanks, Champ. It's always good to have you in my corner. Claire, you heard him. I'm just going to ask. Will you marry me? *Us*?"

## Epilogue

"Always a bridesmaid," Marylou said on a sigh as she handed Chessie a bouquet of petite purple calla lilies. "You're in a rut, darling."

"I know. I've got to start carrying more brides-maid gowns. We're just lucky I had these two on hand, because I didn't have the time to order them. You look pretty good, by the way, Ms. Matron of Honor."

Marylou went over to the mirror and inspected her appearance in the dusky violet gown. "I do, don't I? I'm not too crazy about that title, Matron, but it's probably better than being the world's oldest brides-maid. At any rate, this will be one night Ted doesn't fall asleep in front of the TV."

"No, no, too much information," Chessie teased her, and then quickly attempted to change the subject. "Have you ever been at a wedding here in Packer Chapel before, Marylou? It's so beautiful, and perfect for a candlelight ceremony."

"Not just anyone can get married here. Wasn't Nick smart to be a Lehigh University graduate?"

Chessie smiled. "Yes, I'm sure that's why he picked Lehigh, just in case he wanted to get married here someday. Come on, we should go join the other bridesmaids."

"In a minute. I want to talk to you for a minute."

"Oh, God, I was afraid of that," Chessie said, shaking her head. "All right, get it over with, whatever it is."

"See how compatible we are? You know just when to give up. I appreciate that. All right, here goes. Claire looks like someone out of a bridal magazine in that gown, doesn't she? We both sure do know how to pick them, the right gown for the right bride. And when we put those two things together—well, I've got a great idea."

"Uh-oh," Chessie said, looking toward the door as if eager to escape. "The last time you told me about a great idea you had, I ended up all but kidnapping poor little Stefano."

"Like you didn't enjoy it," Marylou said, dismissing Chessie's protest with a wave of her hand. "No, what I'm thinking is, if we could help Claire slap together a wedding like this in six short weeks, then we're sadly wasting our talents if we stop with just Claire's wedding. I think we ought to expand the business. Still Second Chance Bridal, but we'll be more of a full-service establishment. Wedding planners. Second chance wedding planners."

"We," Chessie repeated. "As in you and me we?"

"Yes, as in partners. People should go with their strengths, Chess, do what they do best. And we're *good* at this."

Chessie didn't want to admit it—and that was an understatement—but Marylou's proposition intrigued her, a lot. "You know, Marylou, that isn't a half-bad idea. Let's talk more about it next week. *Now* can we rejoin the others? Claire's walking down that aisle in five minutes."

"Not yet. I've got another question, as long as I've got you here. Are you going out to dinner with him, or not?"

There was no sense pretending she didn't understand the question. And clearly Marylou had planned the timing of that question so that she had to answer it or else throw Claire's wedding into chaos. "You are a mean and twisted woman, Marylou."

"Yes, I know. So? You can't really go out to dinner with him. I mean, not unless you're planning to dump the soup course over his head."

"I never should have told you Rick called me. But he's only going to be in town for a few days," Chessie said, edging toward the door. "Where's the harm? I mean, he just wants to apologize."

"Oh, honey, no, he doesn't. I don't know what he wants from you, but it isn't a chance to crawl on both knees, asking your forgiveness. You can't go."

"We'll talk about this another time, too," Chessie said, heading for the door. "Besides, can I help it if I'm curious?"

"And you know what curiosity did to the cat," her friend reminded her as they rejoined the others in the larger room.

Chessie put down her flowers and walked in a full circle around Claire, inspecting the gown for any problems. As if a gown like this, worn by a woman like Claire, could present any problems. "Nope, I can't see a thing I'd change. You're perfect."

"I feel like a fairy-tale princess," Claire confided quietly as Marylou handed her a bouquet of miniature ivory calla lilies, only slightly larger than the nosegays the bridesmaids would carry. "Thank you. I never thought I could feel this way. There's just something so *right* about everything. I'm not even nervous. Not a single butterfly. Although I can't wait to see Nick. Isn't that remarkable?"

"It's time, we need to line up for the processional," Claire's father said, poking his head into the room. "I found your ring bearer in the Men's Room, trying to put his suspenders back on. Why he took them off remains a mystery, but he's ready now. Right, buddy?"

Nick's son stepped into the room, his hair a little

stiff where someone had slicked it down with a wet comb, it appeared, and looked at Claire, his eyes wide with wonder. "Wow," he said, and then grinned. "Dad's going to go *nuts*."

"See? Out of the mouths of babes. We're good at this," Marylou whispered to Chessie as they took their places in line, just as the organist began the traditional Wedding March.

The soft light from dozens of candles lit the chapel as Chessie stood in her place and turned to watch the bride make her way down the aisle on her father's arm.

Claire was a beautiful woman. She'd been especially beautiful waiting to walk down this aisle and marry Nick.

But when she'd seen him, waiting for her, Claire Ayers became, for that one special moment, the most beautiful woman in the world. And then Chessie tore her gaze from her new friend's radiant face to look at the groom, see his reaction.

Nick, bless him, had tears in his eyes. What had Marylou said to her that day in the salon? Yes, she remembered. She'd said that Nick had cried *the way a really caring man cries. Honest…real. Not a question in my mind—he's a keeper.*

Chessie loved her job, but every day she was reminded that it wasn't the gown. It wasn't the flowers or the church or the band at the reception or the exotic honeymoon. It was the man. It was the woman.

Nick and Claire knew that, and their belief in each other, their trust in each other and the love they so obviously shared, lit up the chapel like a thousand suns.

*Yes,* Chessie told herself as she dabbed at her moist eyes with the tissue she'd hidden in her flowers, *I believe in second chances. I do...*

\* \* \* \* \*

*Fans of Kasey Michaels'*
SECOND-CHANCE BRIDAL *series*
*won't want to miss Chessie's story,*
*coming in spring 2011*
*from Silhouette Special Edition!*

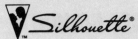
*Silhouette*®

# COMING NEXT MONTH

## Available June 29, 2010

SPECIAL EDITION

**#2053 McFARLANE'S PERFECT BRIDE**
**Christine Rimmer**
*Montana Mavericks: Thunder Canyon Cowboys*

**#2054 WELCOME HOME, COWBOY**
**Karen Templeton**
*Wed in the West*

**#2055 ACCIDENTAL FATHER**
**Nancy Robards Thompson**

**#2056 THE BABY SURPRISE**
**Brenda Harlen**
*Brides & Babies*

**#2057 THE DOCTOR'S UNDOING**
**Gina Wilkins**
*Doctors in Training*

**#2058 THE BOSS'S PROPOSAL**
**Kristin Hardy**
*The McBains of Grace Harbor*

# REQUEST YOUR FREE BOOKS!

## 2 FREE NOVELS PLUS 2 FREE GIFTS!

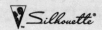

# SPECIAL EDITION
### Life, Love and Family!

**YES!** Please send me 2 FREE Silhouette® Special Edition® novels and my 2 FREE gifts (gifts are worth about $10). After receiving them, if I don't wish to receive any more books, I can return the shipping statement marked "cancel." If I don't cancel, I will receive 6 brand-new novels every month and be billed just $4.24 per book in the U.S. or $4.99 per book in Canada. That's a saving of 15% off the cover price! It's quite a bargain! Shipping and handling is just 50¢ per book.* I understand that accepting the 2 free books and gifts places me under no obligation to buy anything. I can always return a shipment and cancel at any time. Even if I never buy another book from Silhouette, the two free books and gifts are mine to keep forever.

235/335 SDN E5RG

| | | |
|---|---|---|
| Name | (PLEASE PRINT) | |
| Address | | Apt. # |
| City | State/Prov. | Zip/Postal Code |

Signature (if under 18, a parent or guardian must sign)

Mail to the **Silhouette Reader Service:**
**IN U.S.A.:** P.O. Box 1867, Buffalo, NY 14240-1867
**IN CANADA:** P.O. Box 609, Fort Erie, Ontario L2A 5X3

Not valid for current subscribers to Silhouette Special Edition books.

**Want to try two free books from another line?**
**Call 1-800-873-8635 or visit www.morefreebooks.com.**

* Terms and prices subject to change without notice. Prices do not include applicable taxes. N.Y. residents add applicable sales tax. Canadian residents will be charged applicable provincial taxes and GST. Offer not valid in Quebec. This offer is limited to one order per household. All orders subject to approval. Credit or debit balances in a customer's account(s) may be offset by any other outstanding balance owed by or to the customer. Please allow 4 to 6 weeks for delivery. Offer available while quantities last.

**Your Privacy:** Silhouette is committed to protecting your privacy. Our Privacy Policy is available online at www.eHarlequin.com or upon request from the Reader Service. From time to time we make our lists of customers available to reputable third parties who may have a product or service of interest to you. If you would prefer we not share your name and address, please check here. ☐

**Help us get it right**—We strive for accurate, respectful and relevant communications. To clarify or modify your communication preferences, visit us at www.ReaderService.com/consumerschoice.

SSE10R

# HARLEQUIN®

## A *Romance*

## FOR EVERY MOOD™

Spotlight on
## Heart & Home

Heartwarming romances
where love can happen
right when you least expect it.

See the next page to enjoy a sneak peek
from Silhouette Special Edition®,
a Heart and Home series.

*Introducing McFARLANE'S PERFECT BRIDE by* USA TODAY *bestselling author Christine Rimmer, from Silhouette Special Edition®.*

Entranced. Captivated. Enchanted.

Connor sat across the table from Tori Jones and couldn't help thinking that those words exactly described what effect the small-town schoolteacher had on him. He might as well stop trying to tell himself he wasn't interested. He was powerfully drawn to her.

Clearly, he should have dated more when he was younger.

There had been a couple of other women since Jennifer had walked out on him. But he had never been entranced. Or captivated. Or enchanted.

Until now.

He wanted her—*her,* Tori Jones, in particular. Not just someone suitably attractive and well-bred, as Jennifer had been. Not just someone sophisticated, sexually exciting and discreet, which pretty much described the two women he'd dated after his marriage crashed and burned.

It came to him that he...he *liked* this woman. And that was new to him. He liked her quick wit, her wisdom and her big heart. He liked the passion in her voice when she talked about things she believed in.

He liked *her.* And suddenly it mattered all out of proportion that she might like him, too.

Was he losing it? He couldn't help but wonder. Was he cracking under the strain—of the soured economy, the McFarlane House setbacks, his divorce, the scary changes in his son? Of the changes he'd decided he needed to make in his life and himself?

Strangely, right then, on his first date with Tori Jones, he didn't care if he just might be going over the edge. He was having a great time—having *fun*, of all things—and he didn't want it to end.

*Is Connor finally able to admit his feelings to Tori,
and are they reciprocated?
Find out in* McFARLANE'S PERFECT BRIDE
*by* USA TODAY *bestselling author Christine Rimmer.
Available July 2010,
only from Silhouette Special Edition®.*

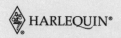

# HARLEQUIN®

## Showcase

LESLIE KELLY
Naturally Naughty

Wicked & Willing

On sale June 8

### Reader favorites from the most talented voices in romance

Save $1.00 on the purchase of 1 or more Harlequin® Showcase books.

---

## SAVE $1.00 on the purchase of 1 or more Harlequin® Showcase books.

Coupon expires November 30, 2010. Redeemable at participating retail outlets.
Limit one coupon per customer. Valid in the U.S.A. and Canada only.

52609057

**Canadian Retailers:** Harlequin Enterprises Limited will pay the face value of this coupon plus 10.25¢ if submitted by customer for this product only. Any other use constitutes fraud. Coupon is nonassignable. Void if taxed, prohibited or restricted by law. Consumer must pay any government taxes. Void if copied. Nielsen Clearing House ("NCH") customers submit coupons and proof of sales to Harlequin Enterprises Limited, P.O. Box 3000, Saint John, NB E2L 4L3, Canada. Non-NCH retailer—for reimbursement submit coupons and proof of sales directly to Harlequin Enterprises Limited, Retail Marketing Department, 225 Duncan Mill Rd., Don Mills, ON M3B 3K9, Canada.

5 65373 00076 2  (8100)0 11654

**U.S. Retailers:** Harlequin Enterprises Limited will pay the face value of this coupon plus 8¢ if submitted by customer for this product only. Any other use constitutes fraud. Coupon is nonassignable. Void if taxed, prohibited or restricted by law. Consumer must pay any government taxes. Void if copied. For reimbursement submit coupons and proof of sales directly to Harlequin Enterprises Limited, P.O. Box 880478, El Paso, TX 88588-0478, U.S.A. Cash value 1/100 cents.

® and TM are trademarks owned and used by the trademark owner and/or its licensee.
© 2010 Harlequin Enterprises Limited

HSCCOUP0610